Embers

Part I

Echoes of Limeville

Published by Pine Veil Press

www.pineveilpress.com

Cover art generated with the assistance of AI, customized by the author

Interior formatting by the author using Apple Pages

ISBN: 979-8-9992839-3-1

First Edition

Printed in the United States of America

Prologue

The morning was pleasant, mild with a teasing warmth that hinted at a summer that hadn't quite arrived—shorts would have to wait for another day. Before setting off, she paused at the edge of the yard, lifted her chin to the sky, and closed her eyes. The sun kissed her cheeks with soft, golden warmth, and behind her eyelids, a kaleidoscope of color danced—reds, oranges, and sparks of violet flickering like a miniature carnival. She twirled in place, arms outstretched, the hem of her shirt fluttering as she windmilled across the yard with carefree abandon, head thrown back in laughter, heart already half in the woods.

Today, she could feel it deep in her bones—was going to be a good day. One of the best.

She gathered her things: a weathered plastic pail packed neatly with wrapped peanut butter and jelly sandwiches, a bag of their favorite chips, two glass bottles of Pepsi clinking gently together, the old metal bottle opener tucked in beside them, and her trusty pink Barbie fishing rod.

1

With a final glance back at the house, she set off toward the tree line.

Sometimes he waited for her. Other times—like today—he'd gone ahead, letting her sleep in while the world quietly unfolded in silver light.

Her small feet, clad in dusty white Keds, padded over the forest floor. Dew still clung to the moss, cool and damp beneath her soles, and the sun had only just begun its climb, filtering through the trees in shimmering shafts that painted the woods in glowing planes of light. Shadows draped themselves loosely across the path, ragged silhouettes shifting gently with the breeze. She knew the way by heart, weaving between trunks and ducking beneath branches, until the trees opened and the clearing welcomed her.

There lay the lake, its glassy surface barely stirred, still cloaked in the breath of morning mist. She'd spent what felt like a thousand days here—fishing, swimming, paddling, and skating when the ice came. It was a lake for all seasons, but spring was her favorite. These early morning hours with him—cool, hushed, timeless—were her secret treasure.

Sometimes they talked: he'd ask about school, her friends, what she'd build with her Legos next. Sometimes she asked about the fish—what they felt, where they went in winter. But often, they simply sat in comfortable silence, lines cast, sandwiches slowly unwrapped with a gentle crinkle of waxed paper, the lake lapping quietly at the shore. They called it "first lunch", with a co-conspiratorial giggle. There was always a second one waiting back home, hunger stirred by hours outdoors. The best days ended with sunburned noses, empty buckets, and full hearts.

She stepped into the clearing, scanning for him.

The blanket was there, spread out just as they always did it, with the small white cooler set atop one corner to keep it from fluttering away. But the space was too still. The cooler hadn't been opened. Her eyes roamed the edge of the sand— and then caught on something that made her breath falter.

A shape in the water.

A body.

There he was. Still gripping his fishing rod, lying face down, fully dressed, his back rising gently with the rhythm of the lake as it cradled him.

Peaceful.
Too peaceful.

"Daddy?" she called, her voice tentative, unsure. He didn't stir. "Daddy?" Louder now, her feet already moving, the pail and rod slipping from her hands and crashing to the sand, Pepsi bottles tumbling and clinking on the ground. "Daddy!"

She ran—ran through the shallow water, splashing up to her hips, her eyes wide and heart pounding, tears streaming hot down her cheeks. She grabbed at his shirt, pulling, straining to turn him over, to lift him, to bring him back to her. He was strangely light and yet impossibly heavy, floating but unyielding, and no matter how she tugged, she couldn't turn him.

He rolled slightly, then drifted back, face still hidden beneath the water.

She let out a choking sob, then did the only thing she could think to do.

4

She ran.

She ran with all the speed her legs could summon, tearing through brush and shadow, leaves clawing at her arms, branches lashing past her face. She didn't stop to breathe or cry. She just ran.

She didn't know what was happening, but she knew it was bad and that she didn't have much time.

She normally loved the feel of the spongy pine needles under her feet—could even feel the soft cushion of them with her shoes on. They were like the mats in gym class that she tumbled on. But today, it felt like, between her wet Keds and the green carpet of needles, they were just conspiring together to slow her down.

She had to get home. She had to get help. She wasn't exactly sure what was going on, but it was not good. Her pounding feet matched that one repetitive, rhythmic thought in her head.

Not good.
Not good.
Not good.

Forever seemed to come and go before she was bursting through the garage door into the kitchen.

Mama was humming with her back to Liz, stirring something in a bowl tucked under one arm. Pancake mix, probably. It was Saturday.

Liz was breathless, still dripping from the waist down and wet-faced. Her mother turned to see what the racket was just as Liz burst into the room.

"Liz! Geez, for crying out loud—" she stopped when she saw her daughter's face. "What's wrong? Elizabeth?" Mama's hand paused in mid-stir as she waited for an answer.

"Dad..." she started. "It's Daddy. He's not moving. He's in the water, and he's not moving!" Liz sobbed the last words out, and before she knew it, the bowl had shattered on the floor, pancake batter splattered across the cabinets, and Mama was out the door.

"Mama!" Liz screamed after her and chased her outside and down the driveway. Mama turned once, her voice bending on the breeze so that Liz had to strain to hear.

"Get your sister and go to Nancy's. Tell Nancy what happened and have her call 911 to get an ambulance down to the lake. Fast. Hurry, Liz. HURRY!"

Liz barely heard the last of her mother's instructions— she was already running full speed down the street toward the woods that led to the lake.

7

Liz ran first to Nancy's. It was the closest house to theirs, and two of Nancy's daughters were about the same ages as Liz and Carrie. Nancy opened the door with an apron on and smiled brightly at Liz.

"Well, honey, aren't you here bright and early! I'm not sure the girls are up yet—" She bent down to meet Liz's eyes and realized the child wasn't there to play.

"What's the matter, honey?" Nancy took Liz's hand and pulled her inside. She crouched down to match Liz's small frame as Liz sputtered out in broken sentences what had happened, then repeated as best she could what her mother had told her.

"Oh my," was all Nancy said before springing to her feet and racing to the phone.

"Go, sweetie. Go get Carrie and bring her back over here. I'll call the ambulance and get them to the lake."

Liz stood, riveted to the wooden floor, watching as Nancy picked up the clunky handset to call 911. After Nancy connected, she glanced back at Liz.

"Go, honey," she said, covering the mouthpiece. *"Go get your sister. It'll all be all right. You did the right thing."*

That was all Liz needed to hear. Her feet snapped back into motion.

She ran home.

Carrie was already standing in the kitchen—one hand clutching her sad, tattered blanket while she twirled a strand of hair with her index finger, the other thumb still planted firmly in her mouth. She stared at the floor, where the broken bowl and pancake batter lay like time had frozen.

"C'mon, Carrie," Liz coaxed. *"Let's go to Nancy's. I'll bet she'll make you pancakes."*

Carrie sniffed and pulled her thumb out of her mouth just long enough to ask, "Wiff bwuebewwies?"

Liz tried hard to smile, the corners of her mouth trembling as she fought to keep it together. Her heart was still pounding, her stomach churning like she might need the barf bowl at any moment, but somehow, she knew she needed to keep her focus on Carrie. I have to stay together for her. I have to. I have to make this right.

"We'll see. C'mon. Let's go." Liz took Carrie's hand gently, leading her out of the house. Carrie kept staring at the mess on the floor, but let herself be guided, her other hand still clutching her blanket, the thumb slowly returning to her mouth as they walked.

Less than five minutes later, after Nancy had changed her into dry clothes, Liz heard the chilling sound of the sirens growing closer. Her heart twisted, a new wave of dread washing over her. She retreated farther into Nancy's house, into the back room with the couch, and pressed her face into the soft pillows. She pulled them tightly over her head, trying to block out the sounds—the sirens, the reality of what was happening. She needed to shut it out. She needed just a little more time before the world came crashing in.

Mama came later. Liz and Carrie were sitting at the table, eating grilled cheese sandwiches and tomato soup, trying to act normal in a house that suddenly felt too big, too quiet. Nancy's daughters, Courtney and Cecilia, sat silently beside them, the weight of the moment hanging thick in the air. Mama walked in through the back door, and Liz saw her immediately. Mama's face was streaked with red, her eyes swollen and hollow, as if someone had ripped the life out of her. She was standing here, but it felt like part of her had gone into the water with him—and didn't come back.

Nancy took her by the hand and led her into the other room. Liz heard soft murmurs, the occasional sniffle and sigh, but the conversation was too low, too quiet to understand. The girls sat there in silence, nibbling their sandwiches, refusing to look at one another. Liz realized they weren't just avoiding eye contact—they were trying to will the bad thing away. If they didn't look, if they didn't acknowledge it, maybe it would disappear.

Finally, Mama came back into the room with Nancy by her side, holding her steady with both hands. Liz watched her mother stand there, one hand over her mouth, her eyes glazed, staring into nothing.

Nancy's voice broke the silence. "Liz, Carrie, are you done with your lunches?" Carrie nodded and got down from the table, seeking the safety of Nancy's ample left arm. Mama didn't move. She stood there, a broken figure in the doorway.

11

Liz, still gripping her sandwich, barely took a bite. She chewed slowly, the food rolling around in her mouth, like she had forgotten how to swallow altogether. She knew, without a doubt, that once she left this table, her world would never be the same. This moment—the quiet before the storm—was the last piece of normal she would ever have. She needed to hold on to it for just a little longer.

I have left the warmth of life behind,

But not the love that tethered me to you.

In every breath you take, I linger—

A shadow in the fold of light.

Grieve if you must, and let the ache move through you,

For sorrow is only love unspoken.

I have not truly gone, my child—

I have only slipped beyond your seeing.

Liz pressed her head into her mother's shoulder, the soft fabric of her mother's blouse warm against her cheek. She breathed in the familiar, comforting scent of her mama's perfume, but today it felt hollow—like it couldn't fill the empty hole inside her. "Tell me again where Daddy is," she whispered, her small voice trembling as she squeezed her stuffed bunny tighter to her chest.

"He's in heaven, Baby. He's watching over you, just like he always promised," Mama replied softly, her voice thick and weary with sadness. She pulled Liz gently away, her hands cupping Liz's face as though she wanted to say more, but instead, tears welled up in Mama's eyes, her grief just too much to bear. She just shook her head, unable to find the words.

Liz, feeling the weight of the moment, knew exactly what came next. She had watched this drill play out over the last several days, the same sad routine where Mama's tears spilled over, and Liz was left to do what she could to hold it all together. She slid off Mama's lap, walking slowly to the box of tissues that always seemed to be somewhere nearby. Her hands were unsure as she handed the box to her mother.

"I don't understand why he couldn't stay here and watch me," Liz said, her words stumbling out in a rush. "Why did he have to go to heaven? Mama, is heaven better than our house? Is there a lake with fish in heaven? Does he have other little girls to fish with there?" She paused, staring intently at her mother, her voice quiet but sharp with the question that had been her constant companion the past couple days, "Doesn't he love us anymore?"

Mama opened and closed her mouth a few times, her lips parting but no words coming out, just like those fish Liz and her daddy caught at the lake. Liz watched her, confused and desperate for an answer, as Mama looked at her, then looked away. But no matter how much Liz waited, no answer came. Instead, Mama's gaze dropped to the floor.

"Go get something to eat, Baby," Mama murmured, dabbing at the mascara that had pooled beneath her eyes. "Mama's gotta go visit with some people."

Liz watched as Mama stood and walked toward the living room, where the crowd had gathered—people from the town, talking in low murmurs, laughing in their own little world. But as soon as Mama entered, the noise stopped. All eyes turned away, down to the worn shag carpet beneath their feet. The silence filled the room, thick and suffocating.

Liz climbed to the top of the stairs and sat at the top, clutching Bunny to her chest as if the softness of the toy could somehow shield her from the heaviness in the air. Her house didn't feel like the same place anymore. Without him, everything felt off-kilter. The house seemed to tilt, like the world had shifted when he'd left. The sunlight streaming through the windows was no longer warm. It was flat, pale, like the real light had gone, and all that was left was a incandescent imitation that didn't quite dissipate the shadows that lurked now. Even the drapes, which had always looked so warm, now seemed dull, washed-out, lifeless. Liz felt like she was stuck in the part of The Wizard of Oz she hated—the part before everything turned bright and colorful, when everything was in black and shades of gray.

She remembered overhearing Mama on the phone, telling people that Daddy had suffered a "heart tack" and drowned. Liz didn't know what a heart tack was, but it sounded like "hard tack," the candy her grandfather used to crunch on and sometimes shared with her. Peppermint stars, butterscotch

16

disks, and sour cherry balls ... *How could something that sounded like candy take away her daddy? Her mind couldn't make sense of it. Her eyes stung, and she pressed Bunny into her face, willing herself not to cry.*

And then there was "drowned." Liz knew what that meant. It meant she hadn't been there, and once she did get there, she had left him in the water. She hadn't done what she should have, what she could have. She hadn't been there to save him. The thought clawed at her insides, sharp and relentless, filling her chest with a cold, suffocating, panicky guilt. It gnawed at her, bitter and unforgiving; an unspoken accusation. How could she live with that? How could she ever forgive herself for walking away when he needed her most?

"Where's Daddy, Bunny?" she whispered into the soft fleece, the question slipping out like a plea. "Why did he leave me?"

She could still feel the warmth of his lap, still remember how he'd hold her there in the big chair by the fireplace. She could smell the faint trace of pipe smoke, the musky scent of the Scotch he drank over ice before dinner. And she could hear his voice—so clear, so certain—telling her, time and again,

17

"You're my special little angel, Lizzy. I will always be here for you. I will always love you."

But where was he now? She peeked out from Bunny's fur and stared up at the ceiling, the place Mama had pointed to when she tried to explain heaven, but it just didn't make sense.

Heaven wasn't real. He wasn't up there. He should have been here, with her, comforting her, like he always promised.

Liz slid off the top step and made her way downstairs again. She had to check his chair. His favorite chair. She needed to see if maybe, just maybe, he was there. But when she peered around the corner, his chair sat empty, just like the rest of the house felt now. Empty.

She stepped closer to the chair, then bent down and touched the fabric, but it was cold. He wasn't there.

Where was he? Her heart screamed his name. DADDY!!

Her chest tightened, and the bitter sting of it all pierced her heart. He wasn't here. He wasn't anywhere.

Daddy lied. And Liz hated him for it. She hated him for leaving her. And she hated herself for letting him go. She wasn't supposed to feel this way. She wasn't supposed to feel abandoned by someone who promised to love her forever. But she did.

She did, and it felt like the biggest, most unforgivable betrayal.

She walked slowly down the aisle, deliberately avoiding eye contact with him. If she'd had any say in the matter, this day would never have happened. She wouldn't be wearing a dusty-rose chiffon gown, holding a bouquet of daisies tied with matching pink satin ribbon, walking toward the man who was about to become her stepfather. He irritated her. He creeped her out. His constant over-attention to her and her sister made her skin crawl. She didn't want a replacement Daddy. She didn't want him at all. And she certainly didn't want to watch her mama laughing and carrying on with, or looking at, another man like she had with her father.

19

Mama had taken her time, and Liz supposed that was okay. Almost five years had passed since her father's death. Mama had only started dating John last year, and Liz hadn't begrudged her mama's happiness. But the truth was, she was just trying to preserve her own. And her happiness had always been built on quiet days with just the three of them. A lot of the days, it had only been her and Carrie, and that was how she liked it.

It wasn't that John was a bad guy—he wasn't. In fact, he was the opposite. He bought her and her sister plenty of gifts, took them out to fancy restaurants where they could order whatever they wanted, and he'd let them get big, sloppy ice cream sundaes for dessert. He wasn't the type to mistreat them. But still, something just didn't sit right. Maybe it was like Aunt Janet had suggested, that Liz just didn't want to share her mama with anyone. Maybe.

The other problem was that he was moving into their house—invading their space. He wasn't just dating her mama anymore. He was settling in. Putting his clothes in Daddy's closet. Sleeping on Daddy's side of the bed. Some days, Liz would see his car in the driveway before the school bus even stopped—his presence already waiting like a shadow stretched across the porch. She'd linger with friends, drag her feet, do cartwheels in the front yard just to buy a few more minutes. Anything to delay walking through that door. It wasn't just the three of them now. And no matter how warm the house looked from the outside, it didn't feel like home anymore.

She had just turned twelve last month. She had seen and experienced more than most twelve year olds. More than any that she'd known. And definitely more than any twelve year old ever should.

Chapter One

The last boxes were coming off the truck.

"In the kitchen, Missus Barton?" the mover asked as he hefted another one toward the porch.

I wiped the sweat from my forehead with the back of my wrist and squinted at the label. *CHINA*.

"Uh, yeah—the counter's fine."

He nodded and disappeared inside with the box like it weighed nothing. I knew better. It held all the serving pieces to my great-grandma's china set, triple-wrapped in newsprint and packing tape.

Across the room, Luke was finishing up with the supervisor—signing papers, writing the check. He glanced up and caught my eye, then winked. I smiled, despite the ache in my shoulders and the fact that I couldn't feel my feet anymore. Even after nine years, he still had that effect on me. A little older, a little rougher around the edges.

I loved those lines near his eyes. They made his face look lived-in—like lines etched with every memory we'd made together.

Funny, the first time I saw him, I wasn't thinking about memories. I wasn't thinking about much at all except how ridiculously hot he looked.

We met at a hole-in-the-wall bar in Ashland. The kind where the walls were yellowed from years of smoke and the table edges had gone soft with time. I was fresh out of Marshall University, still clinging to the comfort of familiar faces, laughing with friends in a corner booth.

Luke, in a worn WVU hoodie, was holding court at the pool table with a bunch of guys. Loud. Confident. And *hot*— the kind of hot that made your drink sweat before you did. I couldn't keep my eyes off him.

Eventually, he wandered over.

"You any good at pool?" he asked, all casual charm.

"I'm exceptional at leaning on the table and looking cute," I replied, raising an eyebrow.

And that, as they say, was that.

I honestly can't remember if my friends were still there by the time I left—or his. We played a game. He won. We talked, flirted, got lost in each other's eyes. And when he walked me to my car, he looked me straight in the eye and said, "I'm gonna marry you someday."

I figured it was just the beer talking. But he'd texted me before I even woke up the next morning, asking when he could see me again.

Now here we were—nine years later, building a life in a place where no one knew our story. But if I let myself stand still too long, my thoughts went straight back to Ashland—and nothing good ever came from that. So I kept moving. One more box. One more piece of our old life settling into this new one.

"Hey, Liz. Where do you want this one, Babe?" Luke asked, stepping through the doorway with a dusty lamp in hand.

I blinked at it like it was a stranger. "Uh... guest bedroom, I think?"

He nodded and headed upstairs, his footsteps echoing in the narrow stairwell.

I turned back to the kitchen and let out a slow breath. The floor creaked under me. The windows rattled a little in their frames when a breeze rolled across the field. The air smelled different here—cleaner, crisper. It was the middle of March, so the wind still had a bite to it.

A fresh start, I told myself. That's what this was.

A clean break.

A fresh page.

And yet.

My chest tightened for half a breath. Not regret exactly. Not sadness. Just the weight of everything I wasn't saying out loud.

I'd told everyone we moved for Luke's promotion. And that was true.

But there was more to it.

More than boxes and job titles and change-of-address forms. It was the ache I carried walking down Main Street back home, the way every set of eyes seemed to know too much.

The forced smiles. The whispers. The pity.

Poor Liz, whose father had drowned.

Poor Liz, whose mother coped with vodka and casual boyfriends.

Poor Liz, still living in the same small town where it all happened, trying to pretend she couldn't hear the echoes.

I didn't want to be her anymore.

The pitied girl with the tragic past. The woman with the grief. The daughter who never got to live her own life without being called selfish.

No, I was done.

Pennsylvania wasn't just a relocation. It was a reinvention. A place where no one knew my name, my past, my story. A place where I could finally breathe without the past snapping open like some wind-up toy I'd forgotten to disarm.

I reached for the next box, arms already aching, and told myself again:

Fresh start.

The door slammed shut behind the last of the movers, jarring me from my quiet thoughts. I felt the familiar knot of stress begin to tighten in my chest again, but then it hit me—Luke and I were finally alone.

The house was ours. I stood there for a moment, taking it all in.

The space. The silence. The newness of it.

I couldn't help but smile to myself, a goofy grin spreading across my face. It was better than I had remembered, prettier, somehow more alive. It had a warmth to it now that hadn't existed in the expertly staged photos I'd studied for weeks.

I'd pinned a photograph of the house's exterior to the wall of my cubicle at work, like a beacon of hope—a promise that this day, this life, could be ours. Every day, without fail, I found myself on the real estate site, scrolling through the pictures of the rooms the previous owners had staged with rented furniture. The rooms had been sparsely, yet impeccably furnished then, and the spaces felt like a dream to me. I'd lose myself in those virtual tours, tracing the edges of the walls, memorizing the angles of each room. I didn't tire of it. I knew each corner by heart.

The kitchen was where my heart truly belonged. Despite the house's 1890 origins, with its classic Pennsylvania farmhouse charm, it was the addition that captivated me the most.

The original structure had been expanded in the early 2000's, with a new eat-in kitchen and a second-floor master suite, but the addition had never been fully completed before tragedy struck in the form of a freak accident that caused a fire. However, the bones of the addition remained, and, just recently, it had been lovingly rebuilt by the previous owners.

They'd brought in a local Amish craftsman to handcraft the cabinets—each one a work of art, the pulls a dark cast iron, every one a little unique in their shape. The plank floors, salvaged from two old churches, had a weathered charm that only age could provide. The maple countertop on the island, rough-hewn by hand, still smelled faintly of wood and earth. Even the stones that graced the fireplace hearth had a history, recovered from a long-abandoned fieldstone barn.

The realtor had pointed out these details during our visit, practically beaming with pride, as though she herself had restored the house. And maybe she had a point. Someone had poured a lot of money and care into preserving the original character of the home while still ensuring it had all the modern conveniences. The result was a space that exuded warmth and homeyness—a place I couldn't resist.

As I reached for the utility knife to open yet another box, Luke appeared in the doorway. His smile was warm, and he leaned casually against the doorframe, his gaze locking onto mine in a way that still made my blood rush a little faster.

"Hey, lover," he drawled, his eyes roaming over me with an intensity that never failed to stir something deep inside me. His gaze had a power to it, a magnetic pull that could have made my clothes fall off with just his look. It still took my breath away, like a swift punch to the solar plexus.

"Hey, yourself." I tucked the utility knife into the back pocket of my jeans and made my way toward him, slowly, deliberately, holding his gaze.

I felt a flutter of excitement as I approached him, enjoying the contrast of my slender frame against his solid, muscular one. I loved that about us.

"You interrupting my work for a good reason, Cowboy?" I slid my arm around his lower back and pulled him a little closer with a quick motion.

"Nah," he said, teasing, and pushed me away lightly. "Just seeing if I could still get your attention. You still want an ol' hillbilly hick like me?" He tilted his head, raising an eyebrow in mock concern.

"Yeah, hey—you're right," I teased back, playing along. "I think I'll trade you in for one of them innocent Amish boys on *Rumschpringe* I've heard so much about." I dropped in a fake country twang, and we both burst into laughter.

The term "*Rumschpringe*," the Amish tradition that allows young people to explore the world before choosing to be baptized, was something I had found amusing—and a little absurd. I had read about it online and shared it with Luke, half-laughing at the idea. Imagining myself as a parent, I couldn't fathom inviting trouble like that.

Luke tapped my backside playfully, "You ready to go get something to eat?"

"Sure." I looked up at him, my chin resting on his chest, still savoring the closeness between us. I wasn't quite ready to let go, but my stomach had other plans.

"What do you have in mind?"

"I don't know," he said with a shrug. "Let's just take a drive and see what's out there. We both could use a break." He leaned down and kissed me gently on the lips, the warmth of his kiss and his soft lips … a promise I savored for later.

By the time we arrived home that evening, the cool night air brushing against us, we were both content, our bellies full from a delightful family-style restaurant we'd found. We vowed to return, over and over again, until it became a staple of our new life.

As the house came into view, Luke sighed.

"I guess it was pretty stupid to leave without turning on a light," he muttered, steering the car toward the porch.

The headlights cast long, stretched shadows across the front door. He gave me a mischievous grin. "I'll stay here. You go turn on the lights—Then I'll park the car."

I raised an eyebrow. "You're scared of the dark, aren't you?"

He grinned. "Terrified. Go save me."

I rolled my eyes, but stepped out into the night. The air was colder than I remembered—sharp, damp. The porch groaned under my feet as I crossed it. I unlocked the door and flipped the switches. Warm light spilled onto the porch and into the front room.

And then the smell hit me.

Faint, but sharp. Damp wood. Smoke. Like a fire that had gone out hours ago but still left the air scorched.

Luke appeared behind me as I stepped further inside.

"Do you smell something in here?" I asked, my nose scrunching as I turned toward the living room, the faintest trace of a scent tugging at me.

Luke, standing just behind me, paused at the threshold before stepping inside. Once the door was securely closed behind him, he took a long breath.

"Yeah... smells like..." He hesitated, his nose twitching as he took in the scent. "Smoke? Wet embers? Like a campfire that has just been doused."

I watched him as he walked around the room, sniffing the air like a bloodhound.

"It's coming from the couch," he said, crouching beside it. "Jesus. What *is* that?"

The smell thickened. Not just smoke. Acrid and bitter — like a campfire that had burned something it shouldn't have. I backed away.

"You think it's something from the move?"

"I don't know. It smells like... burned fabric. Or hair."

My stomach twisted. "Maybe something got packed in it. Something dead?"

He pulled back the cushions. We both stared at the exposed space beneath.

Empty.

"Nothing."

"Okay," Luke said, straightening himself abruptly, palming the back of his neck. "Whatever it is, we'll deal with it tomorrow. Are you ready to go rummaging through those boxes upstairs for some sheets?"

He tacked on a mischievous grin as he raised his eyebrows suggestively. "I'm pooped, but not so pooped that I'm not looking forward to christening this new house with my wife!"

"I already made the bed up earlier, so go ahead," I answered, distracted. "I'm just going to sit here for a moment and enjoy the quiet." I stretched up on my toes to linger in a kiss, feeling the weight of the moment, and that seemed to chase away the lingering doubts that had clouded my mind.

"Wait up for me, though. I'll be up in a few," I added, winking at him with a playful grin of my own.

Luke laughed, and we both shared an unspoken understanding, the giddy excitement of a new chapter in our lives hanging in the air.

My fingers grazed the armrest of the matching overstuffed chair as I let myself sink into the cushions, taking in the soft stillness of the house. The room, empty of the noise of a busy day, felt like a sanctuary. The beauty of the space we had just acquired was starting to settle into me like a gentle hum.

The quiet was comforting, and I felt a deep sense of pride swell within me. We had done this.

This was our place.

Our sanctuary.

Chapter Two

I awoke in the early morning with a jolt, one of those whole-body twitches that you sometimes get as you're falling asleep, but I looked at the clock. It was 5:20 in the morning. I nudged at the big pile of blankets next to me, "Luke. Luke, wake up."

"What? What is it?" He sat up quickly and switched on the bedside lamp.

"Do you smell that?" I asked as I shielded my eyes from the light and sniffed the acrid air.

Luke took a moment or two to come around before he answered me. "Yeah. What the hell *is* that? It smells like that same smell from last night, only stronger. Ugh! Open a window or something," Luke commanded, waving his hand in front of his face.

"I'll go check the house and see what's going on," Luke disappeared out the bedroom door as I swung my legs over the side of the bed and padded over to the window. I unlatched the lock and tugged on the sash.

Nothing.

I stood on my tiptoes to ensure I had indeed unlocked the window and tried again.

It wouldn't budge.

So I tried the other window.

Same result.

"Agh, crud. Damn windows are stuck," I spat at the air.

I grimaced as I pulled again and busted a fingernail.

As I sucked on the sore digit, and buried my nose in my shoulder to try and mask the smell, I directed Luke who had returned from his search, "You try 'em."

Luke gave me his mock salute, laced his fingers together to crack his knuckles and kissed my temple as I stepped aside.

He relocked then unlocked the window.

"Seems to only smell in here, the rest of the house is fine," he shared as he grunted trying hard to free the sash.

He rested his hands on the sill below and tilted his head up to scrutinize the parting bead on both sides of the window to see if there was an impediment there causing it to jam.

"Damn. I'm gonna have to jimmy 'em open, I guess. They must be painted shut or something."

By then I had decided that I needed to escape the concentrated smell of what we could only associate with water soaked campfire embers. It filled my nostrils and was making me sick to my stomach.

"I guess I'm up now," I announced unhappily. I headed to the bathroom to brush my teeth. When I returned from the bathroom several minutes later, I stopped in the middle of the room and sniffed the air again.

"Is it my imagination, or is it gone now?"

"What?" Luke asked, turning around from his seated position on the bed, tugging off his socks.

"That smoke smell," I was still sniffing the air. "I don't smell anything anymore."

"Huh," he breathed in. "Me neither. Weird. Maybe it was coming from something outside." He got up and headed to the bathroom. "I'll be down in a bit. I'm gonna grab a shower, then I'll look around out there."

I stood there for a moment, unsure whether I felt relief or unease. It was gone. But it had been so real, so close...

The weirdness of it still hung in the air like a shadow, and I wasn't sure if I felt better or just more confused.

Luke found me twenty minutes later in the family room, sitting on the coffee table in the middle of a chaotic mess. The utility knife in one hand, my father's broken photo in the other.

The room felt suffocating, like the air itself was thick with something wrong.

"What happened here?" Luke's voice cracked the silence, but there was no anger in his tone—just concern, mingled with confusion as he scanned the room.

I glanced over at the mess of ripped boxes, their flaps smeared with dark, thick smudges. My stomach twisted. "Did you try and unpack some boxes in the middle of the night?" My voice sounded small, hopeful.

Almost like I was asking the question more for myself than him, hoping for an explanation that would somehow make sense.

"Yeah, right," Luke chuckled, but it didn't reach his eyes. He followed my gaze to the open boxes, their contents spilling out like the house had just belched up the last ten years of our lives—items that had been carefully packed, now shattered and scattered across the floor. Some were still wrapped in newsprint, but others had been torn open with no regard for the care I'd taken. Someone had obviously been in here, rifling through our things, and we had no idea what for or how we slept through the noise.

I looked down at the photo in my hands, the one that I had always kept with me —my dad at the lake, young and alive, caught mid-laugh like he didn't have a care in the world. His smile wasn't for the camera. It was for whomever was behind the viewfinder. I used to think that picture held the truest version of him, the one untouched by what came later. He was mine in that moment. And I had always held that picture close, like it held the essence of who he was before death crept in and stole him from me.

The lake was his place. It was where he felt free. And I had always known, even as a kid, that there were two versions of him: the dad that belonged to the steel mill, and the dad that belonged to me, on weekends by the water.

I pulled the photo closer to my chest, as though holding it tighter could protect it from the madness around me, the growing knot of fear I could feel tightening in the pit of my stomach.

"What is going on, Luke?" The words came out in a rush, like they'd been waiting to burst. My chest was tightened, the all too familiar squeeze building again. My eyes were filling, and I could feel it all slipping away—the dream of the perfect escape, my new refuge, the one that was *supposed* to exist, just slowly unraveling.

"I don't know," Luke replied, running a hand through his hair in frustration. "But someone's messing with us." He was pacing now, his voice rising slightly. "Do you think... I don't know, that there were squatters here? This place sat empty for so long, maybe they stayed in here when it was vacant. Maybe the smoke smell came from them trying to keep warm—building fires in the house, because the heat was turned off. This part of the house is old. The dampness, the wind... it could explain the smell, I guess." He stopped, leaning over one of the boxes. His fingers brushed over the black marks again. "But this … it doesn't make sense if they didn't take anything. Why would they break into the boxes like this?"

I didn't have an answer. I just stood there, trying to breathe through the feeling of dread that pressed down on me.

Luke looked up at the ceiling as though it might reveal something to him. "I think we must have some kind of unwelcome visitors," he paused, musing, "yet there are no burn marks or signs of actual fire. It's... strange." He pulled up one of the rugs, inspecting the floorboards

"Hmph," he muttered, shaking his head. "That's the best theory I've got right now."

I dropped my head, still clutching my father's photo. My thoughts felt like a jumbled mess, and I couldn't stop the spinning in my head. This was too much. Too much change, too much chaos, all at once. Luke walked over to the door, muttering to himself about locks, alarms, and the need to secure the house.

"First thing we're doing today," he said, already back into problem-solving mode, "is changing out all the door hardware. Deadbolts on every door, even though these look brand new," he said as he inspected the door. He shook his head, "But who knows who could have keys. Motion detectors for the outside lights," he pointed to the outside, then put his finger to his lips in concentration. "And I'll check all the smoke detectors too." He punctuated the air with the same finger.

"And I'll call about getting a security system set up after the weekend," Luke added, glancing at me. "You were right—being on this busy road, we need to be more careful." He paused. "Also, maybe you could pick up some air fresheners? Those plug-in ones, and some cans of spray for the smell."

I nodded, not really listening. My mind was elsewhere, still stuck on the picture of my dad, the strange feeling that something was wrong, and the unsettling suspicion that things were only going to get worse. And just like that, hope tore loose inside of me, spilling out like floodwaters through a broken dam.

I blinked back tears and tried to redirect my attention to something I could control. And then remembered the odor from last night—the smell of the couch that seemed to have come from nowhere. I walked over to it now, my fingers tracing the fabric, my nose hovering just above it.

"Huh," I muttered to myself, scrunching up my nose. "Smells fine now."

Luke didn't respond. He was already deep in thought, running through his mental checklist for what needed to be done. But I couldn't shake the feeling that something wasn't right. The memory of my dad—his carefree, joyful face at the lake—seemed farther away than ever now. It belonged to a life that had been taken from me long before that photo ever got broken.

Chapter Three

I watched Luke get ready on Monday morning for his first day at work with a near-constant sensation that an iceberg had taken up residency in my chest. Over coffee and a bowl of cornflakes, he pointed his spoon to the ceiling, motioning to our bedroom directly above, as he crunched his latest bite.

"So," he said around the crunch, "you haven't said. How are you sleeping up there?" The question landed softly, but it echoed.

We'd talked about it before buying the place—the fact that the house was on a major road. Luke had even mused about needing earplugs. A two-lane road, sure, but trucks rumbled past like clockwork, steady and unbothered through the night. I'd voiced my concerns, of course—said I might struggle to fall asleep with all the noise. But what I hadn't told Luke, what I couldn't quite put into words, was that the sound had turned into something strangely comforting. Like the trucks were sentries on patrol, guarding our little home from the dark. The noise made me feel less alone. Less... noticed.

I stirred my coffee. "Not bad," I said finally. "Helps that I'm collapsing into bed every night after unpacking. And I guess the house being set off the road a bit makes a difference."

My voice didn't match my words. It carried too much weight, too much weariness. Luke didn't say anything—he just held his spoon in midair and looked at me for a long beat. The way his brow creased made it clear: he wasn't buying all of it.

And he knew it wasn't just the road. The weekend had done something to me. Something about the way the boxes were exploded open in the living room, fragile things shattered —photos, keepsakes, pieces of a life we'd built carefully.

And the smell. God, the smell. Not constant, not even wholly identifiable—just a shifting, creeping presence — a bitter, scorched scent clinging in the air and drifting through the house like it belonged more than we did. One minute it was there — charred and ashen and strange. The next, gone without a trace.

But the worst part? Saturday. When Luke came back from the hardware store with a crowbar in hand, ready to muscle the bedroom windows open. We'd both struggled with them earlier—jammed tight like they'd been painted shut decades ago. And yet, hours later, with the metal bar still untouched, those same windows slid open like silk. Effortless.

That was the moment I felt something in me really start to fray. Like I couldn't keep pretending it was just bad luck or old house quirks. Like something was... seeing how far it could push us.

"You've got to be kidding me." I shot Luke a look that landed somewhere between disbelief and blame.

"What?" he had said, holding up his hands. "It's not my fault they're opening now. It's warmer now." He sounded like he was trying to convince himself. "You'd think the wood would be more swollen now, though, with the sun on it."

He paused then, distracted by a splinter in his thumb. After a half-hearted shrug, he leaned against the window frame, arms folded across his flannel shirt. He exhaled hard, like maybe the house owed him an explanation. Then he stared up at the ceiling, lost in thought.

I glanced upward too, just in case he'd spotted something I hadn't. Nothing. When our eyes met again, he smirked.

"This house has an agenda", he posed. When he saw my brow furrow at him, he continued, "I'm serious, Liz. It's like it has its own mind, its own rules. It's been here way longer than we have—it has seen way more things. Maybe it's trying to teach us something."

He uncrossed his arms with theatrical flair, like a magician revealing a trick. "What do you think? Haunted, or just wise beyond its years?"

I raised an eyebrow, unimpressed. "Not buying it, honey. Not even a little. But A+ for effort."

I pushed myself off the edge of the bed, stretched lazily, and left the room, leaving Luke and his nonsensical musings behind.

At breakfast, the scrape of Luke's spoon in his empty bowl pulled me back from my drifting thoughts.

"So," he said, too casually. "What are you planning to do today?"

His tone was a shade too cheerful, like he was nudging me toward a productive distraction—something to keep me from dwelling on the weirdness of the past several days.

I thought about it for a second. "Not sure. I'll keep unpacking, obviously." I hesitated. The idea of spending the whole day alone in this house made my skin crawl. "Might run to the paint store, pick out some colors for the downstairs. And since you got the WiFi working this weekend, maybe I'll start looking for a job online. Might grab a paper too, see what's out there."

"You remember there's no rush, right?" he said gently. "We talked about you taking some time. Settle in, knock out a few house projects first."

He paused, then added, "And maybe… start thinking ahead. I mean, this could be a good window for us. To try again. Or explore other options. You've got time now—maybe that's a sign."

He said it lightly, like a casual thought, but his eyes didn't waver from mine.

I didn't answer right away. I just smiled and nodded, pretending to stir my cereal. But something in my chest tightened—hope, fear, grief, I couldn't tell.

He wasn't wrong. That had been the plan. And at the time, I'd wanted some time off. After years of working nonstop —two jobs through college, hustling through the early years of our marriage to kill off my student loans—it sounded like a dream. Finally a break. A chance to just be. As for the other thing … I couldn't go there with him now. Not yet.

Especially now. With everything going on in this house? I was restless. And a little spooked. The idea of idle days stretched out in front of me like a dare.

"I know," I finally answered, noncommittal.

He gave me a knowing nod. He could already tell my mind was made up. That was the rhythm of our marriage— he'd share his thoughts, I'd consider them, then often go my own way. Not to be difficult. I respected him, truly. But I needed to feel in charge of my own choices. We'd never said that out loud, but we both understood it and it worked for us.

Before he left for work, I reminded him—again—to call about the alarm system. He kissed me goodbye, then jogged down the steps and slid into the car.

I leaned against the doorframe, arms folded, and watched him pull onto the busy street, already missing the comfort of his presence in the house that was suddenly too quiet.

After he left, I wandered back to the kitchen table, still cradling my coffee. The steam had thinned, the silence folding in around me.

He hadn't said much—just that I had time now. That maybe this was the moment to start thinking ahead. To try again.

The words had been soft. Hopeful.

But they still landed like a stone.

Tilting my head back, I stared at the ceiling and let memory settle over me like dust.

It was less than a year ago. We were in the middle of one of those late-night conversations—the kind where the glow of the lamp felt gentler than the things being said.

"We're not getting any younger," Luke had said, rubbing the back of his neck as he leaned against the kitchen counter. "I just think... maybe it's time to move forward. Like really move forward."

I'd said nothing. Just watched the way the light caught the silver threading into his hair.

"I mean, we've tried. For over a year now. You and I both know something's not clicking. I'm not giving up—I just think we should talk about... options."

That word. Options. He always said it like it was a gift —like possibility itself.

But to me, it sounded like pressure dressed up in hope.

I hadn't said much that night. I'd nodded in all the right places. I'd let him talk, let him paint the future in broad, hopeful strokes. Donor eggs. IVF. Adoption. It all spilled out of him with a kind of bright energy I couldn't match.

He had so much faith in next steps. In science. In solutions.

I had faith in silence. In waiting. In nature doing what it was supposed to do, or not doing it, and letting that be the answer.

In private, I'd tried to believe. I took the pills, I tracked the temperatures, I learned more than any human should ever have to know about things I didn't especially want to know about.

Every morning began with a thermometer. And every month ended with disappointment.

When he started using words like injections and egg-retrieval, I found myself shrinking from the conversation. Not because I didn't want a baby—I did. Desperately. But the idea of coaxing one into existence through lab visits and needles and calendars made me feel like I was stepping into something too engineered, too clinical. Like I was crossing an invisible line I couldn't articulate, even to him. I wasn't against it, necessarily. But I wasn't ready to embrace it either. So instead, I went quiet. I let him talk. I nodded. And inside, I stalled.

We hadn't fought exactly. But we hadn't agreed, either. Not really. We were standing at the same crossroads, facing opposite directions. I didn't think he saw it yet.

Back in the quiet of the kitchen, I blinked against the burn behind my eyes. One tear escaped before I could stop it. I wiped it away quickly, annoyed at myself. This wasn't the time for tears. That movie had played before. I knew all the scenes by heart.

Then the job offer had come—like a lifeline folded in a manila envelope.

It felt like permission. A sanctioned pause. We had stayed up late for weeks, weighing the move—running through lists, costs, neighborhoods, possibilities. I told him it was the right call. He agreed. We were excited. On paper, it made so much sense.

But secretly, I'd felt something else too: relief.

Relief that we could put the family conversation on the shelf for a while. That I could stop nodding. That the space between what he wanted and what I could give wouldn't have to stretch any further—for now.

It bought me time. And now, it seemed, time was up.

The phone vibrated on the table—its first buzz since we'd moved in—and it startled me more than it should have. I stared at it for a long second, feeling strangely hesitant, before turning it over and checking the caller ID.

Carrie. Relief swept through me.

"Liz!" my sister's voice burst through the line like sunshine.

"Oh my God, hi!" I said, nearly breathless, almost letting the dam overflow with the sound of her sweet voice.

"How was the move? How's the house? Do you love it? Have you met any neighbors? What's the weather like? Did you—"

"It's fine," I said, cutting in, not entirely convinced she'd ever stop with the torrent of questions if I didn't interrupt. My words dropped out flat, like day-old coffee.

Carrie paused. That pause that only a little sister can pull off—half concern, half suspicion. "What the...? You okay? You sound weird. Are you just wiped out?"

I hesitated, then let the entire weekend tumble out in a breathless ramble—roving smoke smells, box contents in disarray, locked windows that opened without effort, uneasy dreams. All of it.

Carrie listened, unusually quiet, until I finally ran out of steam.

"Whoa. Okay. So like... are you thinking it's haunted?" Her voice lifted with more intrigue than fear.

There it was. Classic Carrie. Always the first to suspect ghosts, fate, divine signs, or curses. Like the time it poured at Donna and Jake's outdoor wedding and Carrie swore it was Donna's dead mother trying to stop the ceremony. "She knew Jake was a cheating douche canoe," she'd said at the reception. "That storm wasn't weather—it was justice."

"You're impossible," I said, laughing softly. "But thanks. Seriously. Just hearing your voice... I didn't realize how much I needed it."

"Well, duh. You moved to the middle of nowhere in a possibly haunted house. You should've packed me in a box."

It came out before I could stop myself. "You should come. I'll buy your ticket—just fly out for a long weekend this weekend."

There was a pause. "Wait. You're serious?"

The idea of her here—her laugh, her presence, her faded sleep shirts with the holes in them that she refused to get rid of —suddenly made the house feel a little less daunting.

"I'll send you flight info later," I said.

A knock came at the front door. I flinched.

"Hey—someone's here. I gotta go." I moved toward the entryway. "Think about it, okay? I'll call you tonight."

"Done. I'm already mentally packing."

I set my phone down on the small hall table and peeked through the peephole.

A woman stood outside—distorted through the fish-eye lens. I cracked the door open, and she immediately extended a dish toward me, pressing it in my hands deliberately, like a peace offering.

"Hi! I'm Shelly," she said breathlessly. "I live—well, kind of next door, if you count a long walk and a blind curve as 'next door.' Down that way." She gestured vaguely west with her chin and a nervous laugh. She looked to be in her mid-thirties, but it was hard to pin down. Her blonde hair was pulled into a ponytail so tight it gave her cheeks a little lift, and her lipstick—bright, a little too perfect—a vivid contrast on her pale skin. She wore a turtleneck with a cardigan inside an old unbuttoned pea coat and her jeans were pressed. Pressed. On a Monday morning. Ugh!

Her eyes were a vibrant, deep blue—just sharp enough to make you feel like she could see things you didn't want seen.

I took the plate—still warm, a crumb looking topping glistening faintly beneath the plastic wrap.

"It's Shoo-fly, a Pennsylvania Dutch specialty," she chirped. "We heard you were from out of town."

I thanked her, fumbling the plate in one hand, and tried to offer a polite smile, but her own expression was... strange. All lips and teeth, like a puppet trying to grin. Too much animation in the face, far too little behind the eyes.

Then she leaned in slightly, craning her neck to peer past me into the house.

I followed her gaze instinctively. Nothing there but boxes. No boogeyman looming in the shadows, no forgotten coat on the banister. Still, my shoulders tensed.

She realized she'd been caught and snapped back upright. "I just wanted to wish you the best. You know... in your new home." She spoke with the rapid, rehearsed cadence of someone who had been over this moment in her head a few times.

She turned to go.

"Wait," I blurted. "You want to come in? I've got fresh coffee."

I said it more out of politeness than hope.

Shelly hesitated, half turning, eyes flicking past me again, like something inside the house still held her interest.

"Another time," she said quickly. "Not today. I've got to... run."

And she did. She practically jogged up the drive, her figure growing smaller as she followed the narrow strip of grass alongside the highway toward wherever her home was.

I stood there holding the pie, one slipper curled against the stone threshold. She hadn't even asked my name.

A laugh escaped me—half amusement, half ...I didn't know what. "Well, that was... something."

I closed the heavy door behind me, the lock clicking louder than expected, echoing in the house. Maybe everyone around here was like that—guarded, a little weird. Or maybe Shelly was just odd.

Back in the kitchen, I set the pie on the counter and opened my laptop to look for flights. If there was one thing I could count on, it was Carrie. She'd drop everything to show up—probably with a sage stick, a bottle of wine, and a flashlight she'd call "ghost insurance."

And somehow, even though money was tight, I knew Luke wouldn't mind.

Chapter Four

Carrie looked around in open-mouthed wonder. "Wait —I thought all the walls were white in the listing photos?"

She spun around to face me, eyebrows raised, and I just smiled at her, soaking in the comfort of her presence. Somehow, having her here made it all feel more normal. More *real*. Like the house was just a house again.

"She's been busy," Luke said, grinning like a proud dad at a science fair. "You know Liz—once she gets an idea in her head, she's all in. I came home from work Monday and the kitchen was already painted, walls and trim."

Carrie gasped dramatically. "I *love* the green in here! And those deep purple accents? It's like… an artichoke. Oh, oh … or one of those Mission figs. In the best possible way." She spun around, already halfway across the room. "And this taupe in the living room with the dark brown trim? Obsessed!"

She was already walking the perimeter, touching things like she might take them home. "Six-inch baseboards? Are you kidding me? And those window sills? You only see those in real colonials." She turned to me with a gleam in her eye. "This place is amazing, Liz. I want to move in." Then, throwing a wink at Luke, she added, "Especially with a ghost on the premises."

She laughed—easy and open, like nothing about this situation was even a little strange.

And then the picture fell.

It started with a subtle scraping sound—just enough to make us look. Our formal wedding photo, perfectly perched on the mantle a moment earlier, gave a visible shudder. Then, almost like it *wanted* to step off the ledge, it rocked forward once, twice… and dropped. Glass-side down. The crash echoed through the room like punctuation.

All three of us froze.

I wrapped my arms around myself, suddenly cold. Luke strode forward after a beat, frowning, inspecting the mantle like he expected to find a culprit. He bent to gather the largest shards without saying a word.

I didn't move. Didn't speak. I couldn't even look at Carrie.

Instead, I turned and walked to the kitchen, retrieved the dustpan and broom, and handed them off to Luke in silence. Then I slipped out the front door.

Carrie found me a few minutes later, standing just off the porch in the yard, arms crossed tightly over my chest, staring up at the gray, indifferent sky like it held all the answers I didn't have.

"Whoa," she said softly. For once, she had no jokes, no quips. Then, trying: "Did I do that?" in her best Erkel impression. Her laugh was thin and uncertain as she nudged my elbow.

She dropped her voice. "Is that the kind of stuff that's been happening?"

I nodded and let out a humorless chuckle, but the smile never made it past my lips. "That's the first time we've seen something happen right in front of us. Before, it was just little things. Stuck windows opening on their own. Boxes being opened. Doors refusing to budge. We thought maybe squatters were getting in—people who used the house while it was empty. We changed the locks and added deadbolts, and things have quieted down a little."

I paused. "Except for the smoke smell. That's still happening. Usually at least once a day. Just… hanging there. No source."

Carrie blinked. "Smoke?"

"Like a bonfire, or maybe burning leaves. Sometimes it's sharp—like it's actually inside. Other times it's faint, like a fire miles away, drifting in on the wind. Just… there. And then gone."

She looked toward the house, then back at me. "Okay. I thought you were crazy before, but now... I'm rethinking my stance."

I finally managed a faint smile. "Welcome to my world."

Luke appeared just then, two coats slung over one arm. He wrapped one around my shoulders and handed the other to

Carrie. She slipped hers on, grateful. I let mine sit there, appreciating the weight of his arms more than the fabric.

"Everything okay in there?" Carrie asked.

Luke gave a short nod. "I think so. That was… weird." He glanced from one of us to the other. "We all saw it move, right? The frame actually rocked back and forth before it fell?"

Carrie nodded solemnly. I couldn't even manage that much.

"I mean… bizarre," Carrie echoed. "Maybe it was a tremor? Is there a fault line near here. Or doesn't Pennsylvania have those lime deposits that cause sinkholes? I swear I read about that somewhere."

Luke gave a noncommittal shrug.

"Or maybe it was a truck rumbling by. Yeah. You might have to bolt some stuff down if it keeps happening."

I didn't say anything. None of us really wanted to consider the more obvious explanation.

Fortunately, the incident faded into the background as the day wore on. Carrie and I busied ourselves with little projects—hanging towel racks, organizing closets, swapping stories as we worked. By the time dusk settled in, the house felt almost normal again.

"Let's go to dinner," I said, brushing my hands on my jeans. "There's this place you *have* to try—Plain and Fancy. Total throwback. Think Mom's Thanksgiving, but served by strangers in bonnets." I explained the experience to her in vivid detail.

Carrie wrinkled her nose. "Community tables? That sounds like a nightmare."

"You'll love it. Cold salads, fresh bread with icing, fried chicken, chicken pot pie, brown buttered noodles, mashed potatoes... it's like eating in a Hallmark movie."

She squinted her eyes at me, caught between skepticism and temptation.

"There's also sausage," I added. "And pie. Shoofly pie."

"Ugh, fine. You had me at brown butter," she groaned, letting me tug her off the chair. "But if I end up sitting next to some guy named Amos who wears suspenders and waxes poetic about his prized turnips, I'm blaming you."

We wobbled back into the house hours later, bloated and delirious with carbs. Carrie collapsed on a stool by the kitchen island, still in her coat, head flopped onto the cool wood like a hungover teenager.

"If I lived here, I'd be the size of this house," she moaned.

She lifted her head just enough to peer at the pie box she had unceremoniously plopped on the counter. "I cannot believe that pie has no fruit. What *is* that sticky brown stuff anyway? Fairy poop?"

I laughed and unwound my scarf. "Molasses, I think. And butter. And probably a thousand calories."

"Sheer magic," Carrie said dreamily. "I'm eating this for breakfast tomorrow with my coffee. Do not judge me."

I picked the pie up and placed it in the refrigerator, and pointed toward Shelly's house.

"You think that one was good? The neighbor who brought over the homemade one? *Ten* times better. If I can get her to stay still long enough, maybe I'll ask for the recipe."

Carrie raised her head. "The awkward one who tried to case the joint?"

"That's the one," I said, smiling. "But hey. She knows her way around molasses and crumb topping. Can't hold that against her."

Luke headed up to bed shortly after. Carrie and I went upstairs to change. While I was in the kitchen readying the coffee for the morning, Carrie strolled back into the kitchen, in a long, ripped nightshirt I swear she'd had since high school and her slippers, carrying two wine glasses by their stems. She plunked them down and held up a bottle with a raised brow.

"Red or red?" she asked.

"Dealer's choice," I chuckled, pulling out the corkscrew from the drawer behind me.

A few minutes later, we were curled up in the living room, the overhead lights off, just the golden halo from the lamp in the corner softly illuminating the room. Carrie swirled her glass and peered into it, as if she were trying find answers in the liquid.

"She's been saying stuff again," she said, almost too casually. "Mom."

I didn't answer. Just took a long sip of wine.

"She doesn't get why you moved so far away. Thinks it's... selfish, I guess. Or impulsive. She said, and I quote, 'Who buys a house in the middle of nowhere when their whole family is right here?'"

I let out a dry laugh. "Classic."

Carrie took a long sip of wine, then swirled the glass slowly in her hand. "Can I ask you something without you biting my head off?"

I smirked. "Depends. Is it about my wardrobe choices? Because I stand by this hoodie."

She gave a soft laugh. "No, I mean… why here? Why this house? And yes … maybe …why so far? I know for a fact Luke had other job offers near Ashland."

I hesitated, staring at the floorboards, at the knots and swirls in the wood like they might offer me an answer. She wasn't wrong.

"I guess I just needed… space."

"From Mom?"

"From everything." I let the words roll out slowly, carefully. "I needed to be somewhere I wasn't constantly holding everything together for someone else. Somewhere I could hear myself think. Somewhere quiet enough to feel anything at all other than what I was feeling … there."

Carrie didn't jump in. She just let it sit, nodding like she'd already known but was waiting for me to say it out loud.

"She also asked me if you'd said anything to me about when you were going to start a family. She said you're 'getting up there.'"

I rolled my eyes, the wine suddenly bitter in my mouth. "Oh, my God. So my uterus is officially on a timer now?"

"She doesn't mean it to be awful," Carrie offered gently. "I mean... it is awful, but I don't think she *means* it."

"She's always been like that, though." I kept my voice even, but I could feel the tightness building under my ribs. "Judgy, clingy, and constantly acting like her passive-aggressiveness is some kind of love language."

Carrie didn't argue.

I set my glass down, maybe a little too hard. "It's not like I haven't thought about it. About kids. I mean, of course I have. We've *been* trying. For over a year now."

Carrie's eyebrows lifted, and she reached for my hand again, but I wasn't done.

"I've peed on so many sticks, I should buy stock in Clearblue. And Luke... he's trying to be upbeat about it. He keeps saying, 'Whatever it takes.' IVF, donor eggs, adoption, whatever." I looked at her, my voice lower now. "And I know he means it. I know he'd love any child that came into our life. But I'm not sure I'm built the same way."

Carrie's face softened. "You're not *her*, Liz," she whispered as if she knew exactly what I was thinking.

"I know," I said automatically. Then quieter, "But she's the model I grew up with. It's hard to imagine being anything else."

"You would be. You already are. You broke the cycle the second you started worrying about that."

I shook my head. "I feel... defective. Like there's a part of me that's missing the mom gene or something."

Carrie nudged me with her shoulder. "There's no gene. There's just love. And if you ever have a kid? That kid is going to be *so lucky*. But also—if you don't? That's okay too. It doesn't make you less."

I blinked at her, throat tight.

She grinned. "Besides, if you do, I fully intend to be the inappropriate aunt who teaches them how to swear in context and buys them candy before dinner."

I smiled, but it faded almost as quickly as it came.

"She called me 'chilly' once. To my face," I added, staring into my glass and changing the subject. "Like, actually used the word, 'chilly'. Said all she wants to do is help, and I push her away."

Carrie's laugh was quiet and rueful. "She said something similar to me when I didn't come home for Easter last year. But you... I think it stings more for her with you. You were always the one she leaned on. Especially after..."

She didn't have to finish. I knew.

After Dad died.

Carrie shifted on the couch and pulled her legs up underneath her. "I barely remember him, you know? I was four. All I really remember is that he smelled like the outdoors and that he used to pick me up like I weighed nothing."

I nodded. "He did the same to me, even when I was too big for it. He'd groan and say, 'You're getting heavy, kiddo,' but he'd always do it anyway."

There was a pause, soft and reverent.

"I think I remember the funeral," Carrie said. "Just flashes. A scratchy dress. Mom crying in the kitchen. And you... sitting, staring with your stuffed animal at the top of the stairs."

I closed my eyes, picturing it like a snapshot in reverse. "I used to pretend he was still out there. That he'd just... forgotten to come home. I'd stay up late, listening for the garage door."

Carrie reached for my hand and held it loosely in hers. "You carry all of it, don't you?"

I shrugged, suddenly tired. "Someone had to. You were so little. And Mom just... fell apart. I didn't have time to."

She squeezed my hand. "You were so young. That wasn't fair."

"Life isn't fair," I said, without venom. Just a kind of flat resignation I wasn't even sure I believed. "But that's what happened."

I paused, then added, quieter, "I used to think if I could just be a better kid—smaller, quieter, less trouble, more polite, whatever—then maybe she'd love me better. See me. Want to spend time with me.

"How sad is that?"

I shook my head, a bitter half-laugh escaping. "But it's not just sad. It's pitiful."

Carrie's eyes welled, and her voice was soft when she said, "I'm sorry. I never knew. You carried it with such grace. You never said anything."

"And I'm angry," I went on, almost like I hadn't heard her—but I had. Her words had landed, they just hurt too much to touch yet. "And it took leaving to finally see it. I had to be on the outside to understand just how much I'd taken on."

I paused, feeling the truth of it settle in. "She never absolved me. Not once. Never said it wasn't my fault. I was a kid, for Pete's sake." My voice cracked, just for a second, before I steadied it again. "And I spent so long thinking it was all my fault."

Carrie didn't argue. She just held on a little tighter.

The silence between us softened, settled.

Then Carrie tilted her head, eyes searching mine.

"Do you ever... feel him? Dad, I mean. Do you ever feel like he sends you messages?"

I blinked, caught off guard.

"Do *you*?" I turned the tables.

Carrie threw her head back and sighed. "I don't even know if I'd know what to look for. I have so little to go on."

She glanced around at the walls of the living room. "Do you think it's him? Here. In the house, I mean."

I paused to consider that for a bit, kind of surprised I'd never asked myself that before.

"No. I don't think it's him. If it were Dad, I'd feel it in my bones—something gentle, comforting. Whatever's here feels heavy, unsettled... almost angry. It doesn't feel like him."

Carrie nodded slowly, and something shifted in her expression—like maybe she was hoping I'd say that.

I looked over her head to the stone chimney behind her. "You know, he promised he'd always be with me." My voice thinned. "But then he left."

I blinked, the words barely out before the rest spilled forward.

"And I think I've been mad at him this whole time, too. I know that doesn't make sense—it wasn't his fault. But he made a promise. And then he broke it."

Carrie didn't rush to reassure me. She just sat with it. Let it be true.

We sat like that for a while, two sisters in the hush of this strange old house, sipping wine and remembering the same man from two very different vantage points—one in flashes, one in shadow.

Then, gently: "Just so you know... I really would make a kick ass aunt."

I laughed. "I know you would. That kid'd be some kind of lucky."

Chapter Five

A heaviness clung to me the morning I drove Carrie to the airport—something thicker than sadness, quieter than grief. Melancholy, maybe. Or its shadow, settling into my bones.

We barely spoke on the way there. I couldn't find words that didn't sound brittle. And when I tried to get Carrie to promise she'd visit again soon, she gave me a look that landed like a soft slap.

"Oh, sweet sister." She pulled my face close, her forehead pressing lightly to mine. "You know I love you more than anything, right?"

I nodded. I already knew what was coming.

"But I don't think I can stay in that house again. Maybe next time we splurge on a bed and breakfast? Spa weekend? Mud masks, massages and room service?" She forced a hopeful smile, but her eyes were already far away.

I stared back at her, mute. Ten years old again. The same silence I used to use as a shield when Mom was mid-tirade, and anything I said would only make it worse. I didn't have the energy to explain, to defend myself, to say *It's not my fault. It's not fair.* Besides, that only rang hollow in my head.

Because truthfully? I couldn't blame her. Not after this morning. This morning had been the final straw.

I'd woken to sunlight already in the room—late. Gloriously, impossibly late. For the first time in weeks, I'd slept through the early hours without waking from dreams or creaking floorboards or that unsettled *feeling.* No phantom footsteps. No smoke smells. No soot, or opened boxes, or broken photo frames. No tug at the edge of my sleep.

The bed was empty. Luke must have slipped out without waking me—rare. Usually, even his smallest shift pulled me back to the surface.

I threw on my robe, did the usual bathroom dash— brush teeth, wash face, pee—and then hurried downstairs, eager to find my sister and soak up every last second I had left with her.

But halfway down the steps, I stopped cold.

The living room was … wrong.

All the furniture had been shoved to one side of the room. The couch, armchair, coffee table—every last piece stacked in a haphazard pile like a child's fort. Lamps balanced on side tables. Picture frames wedged between sofa cushions. The area rugs weren't folded or rolled, just kicked into loose heaps along the wall, like something had moved through in a hurry.

For a second, the sight tugged at something old. A memory.

We'd done something like this once. After Dad died. She sat on the stairs in her footie pajamas while I dragged every cushion and blanket I could find into the middle of the living room, building something—anything—that might make her smile. Mom had locked herself in the laundry room, sobbing. I remember thinking maybe if I could make it feel magical, I could make it stop hurting.

I blinked, trying to shake the thought loose. The scene in front of me wasn't warm or playful. It was… wrong.

I tilted my head, then again the other direction. *What the actual hell.*

It looked like someone had cleared a space for dancing. Or summoning something.

I twisted my fists over my eyes, gave my head a little shake, and blinked again. Still there. Still absurd.

Was this some weird plan? A joke? My sister's idea of fun?

I walked into the kitchen, not even trying to hide my confusion. Luke and Carrie were at the table, hunched over their mugs, talking low. They stopped when they saw me.

I hovered in the doorway, uncertain.

"Nice redecoration," I croaked finally, trying to sound amused. "But I think I liked it better the other way."

My laugh—meant to break the tension—hung in the air like a cobweb. I actually swiped the air in front of me like I could clear it away.

They didn't laugh.

Carrie stared into her coffee like she was reading tea leaves. Luke looked like someone had just walked in on him with his hand in the proverbial cookie jar. He gestured stiffly to the empty seat beside him.

I didn't sit.

"What's going on?" My voice was sharper than I intended. "Did something happen? Did you two..." My throat tightened. "Was there an argument? What is this?"

Still nothing.

So I poured my own coffee—hands trembling just enough to spill a few drops—and finally sat down. I stared at Luke until he met my eyes.

He sighed. "We were hoping it was you," he said quietly.

"Hoping *what* was me?"

"That you'd moved the furniture," he said. "That maybe you'd woken up in the middle of the night, had a burst of inspiration... or something."

He winced at his own words.

"I came downstairs first," he continued. "Saw the mess. Thought maybe you and Carrie were up late, got a wild hair, started rearranging things and just... left it. But when Carrie came down and was just as surprised, we both kind of landed in the same place."

He glanced at her. She didn't look up.

"No one remembers doing it. No sore muscles. No bruises. Nothing to suggest sleepwalking or midnight weightlifting. So..." he shrugged helplessly, "here we are."

I stared at him, then at Carrie, then back again at him like a silent tennis match, waiting for one of them to crack a grin. *Please let this be a prank. Please let someone break.*

But their expressions didn't budge.

"Holy shit-balls," I whispered. "You're serious."

No one laughed.

Later, at the airport, Carrie held my hand a little longer than usual. We hugged tighter

"Mom would probably say that house has bad energy," she said with a roll of her eyes and a half-smile. "But I'll just say… trust your gut, okay?"

She looked at me then, more serious. "And promise me —if it ever feels worse than weird, if it crosses that line from unsettling to unsafe… you'll leave. You'll get out."

I opened my mouth to deflect, but she cut me off.

"I mean it, Liz. Don't wait for proof. Don't try to rationalize it. Just go."

I nodded, the lump in my throat making it hard to speak.

She didn't say she was scared. She didn't have to.

The drive back from the airport was all sunshine and open windows. Even though there was still a chill in the air, I turned on the heat to full blast and slid open the sunroof to soak in the light, blasted some tunes from my phone hooked to the car, and sang along—loud, off-key, and with a few lyrics I made up on the spot. It was absurd, but it worked. For a few miles, at least, I felt like myself again. Maybe even better than that—a version of myself I hadn't been since we moved.

I laughed out loud as I butchered a chorus and grinned like a fool. For the first time since we'd arrived, I could actually see the beauty in the rolling hills of Lancaster County.

White clapboard farmhouses and red barns dotted the landscape, tucked among neatly stitched fields that spread out like a quilt. Yards held horses, cows, sheep, or goats, grazing lazily beneath wide skies. Laundry flapped on clotheslines— black pinafores and trousers paired with navy and dark purple shirts, the quiet uniform of the Amish.

Every so often, traffic slowed behind a black buggy pulled by a trotting horse. I always tried to sneak a glimpse of the riders—bonnets, beards, and that stare ahead austerity they carried like a birthright.

It made me wonder, again, what it would feel like to live that simply. No phones, no news alerts, no constant grasping for more, more, more.   I wasn't immune to the consumer hunger—I'd practically memorized the outlet mall brochure that came in our welcome packet—but lately, the idea of that simple life had begun to feel less like deprivation and more like a refuge.

The main roads wound through postcard towns—Intercourse, Paradise (next to Intercourse.   Yes, really. Geography is poetic.), Blue Ball, Bird-in-Hand, Fertility, Lititz —and yes, I still chuckled every time I heard those names. Carrie had nearly fallen off the couch when I had first told her about them.   She made me pull out the map and prove it, and then demanded we hit every one of them, just so she could say she'd been there.

But by the time I turned onto our road, the warmth began to drain. It was like driving through a curtain of shadows. My fingers tightened on the wheel. The house loomed ahead, sunlit but somehow still somber. It didn't matter that it was a perfect spring day. It didn't matter that I'd just laughed until I cried belting out nonsense lyrics to Taylor Swift.

As I pulled into the driveway, that familiar weight crept back in—low and cold and unwanted. The air felt thicker here. Heavier.

I wasn't ready to be alone in that house again.

So I grabbed my purse and started walking.

Instead of heading toward Shelly's place, I turned east. I wasn't in the mood for another pie ambush or any tight-lipped small talk. The next house was farther off the road, nestled behind a row of sugar maples that hadn't quite leafed out. As I approached the porch, the front door creaked open.

A woman stepped out. Small. Sturdy. The kind of short that made you take note.

For half a second she simply stared. Her smile stalled mid-rise, as if she'd stepped through a time warp and needed a breath to place me.

Her eyes flicked over my face, widening—not with fear exactly, but something sharper, older. Recognition.

"I saw you coming," she said at last, the smile catching up. "You must be the new neighbor."

"I am," I said, surprised by how quickly I warmed to her. "I'm Liz."

Something crept into her eyes—was it relief? Recognition?—before she smiled. "Well, Liz," she said, holding out both hands, "I'm Anna. Come in, come in. I just made some coffee."

She was dressed in a red gingham apron, knotted high around her waist over gray polyester pants that stopped just at her ankles. Her hair was a fluffy white cloud, gently crimped, with the telltale dents of a weekly wash-and-set. She looked like someone you'd see on the label of molasses or homemade jam. Familiar, safe.

But her eyes—pale and watery blue—watched me with more intensity than her smile let on.

I followed her into the house, draping my jacket over the smooth curve of a walnut banister. I couldn't help trailing my fingers along it—buttery soft from decades of touch, worn down to a velvety patina. The steps matched the railing: walnut treads with white risers, that I just knew would feel solid beneath my feet.

The house felt like a museum to another time. Heavy wood furniture. Handwoven rugs. Wrought iron light fixtures. Big wooden cookie molds and hand-dipped candles atop of old wooden spools. In the living room, a full-size loom filled one corner, and across from it, a spinning wheel rested like it had been set there mid-use, a crude basket holding clumps of colorful woolen yarns at its feet. It was beautiful. Albeit a bit cold.

A chill snuck under my skin, enough that I missed my jacket the moment I let it go.

The kitchen was no less striking. Walnut cabinets, weathered and proud. Oak butcher block counters. A brick floor laid in herringbone. And dominating one wall, a walk-in fireplace blackened with soot, an iron cauldron hanging over cold ash. Tools—bellows, pokers, long-handled ladles—all hung from a rough hewn wooden mantel and hand-wrought iron hooks, like relics waiting to be remembered.

It was breathtaking. And a little unsettling. Like the past hadn't left. Not completely.

"Sit," Anna said, her voice bright again. She poured coffee into two well-worn plain Pfaltzgraf mugs and paused. "Milk?"

"Just black, thanks," I held up my hand, my eyes still sweeping the room.

When she set the mug in front of me, her fingers brushed mine. She flinched—just a micro-jolt—and muttered, almost under her breath, "Lord, the likeness…"

I blinked. "I'm sorry?"

"Nothing, dear," she said quickly. "Just déjà vu catching up with me."

I took a sip of coffee, grateful for something warm to hold. The silence that followed wasn't exactly uncomfortable, but it left a faint static in the air—like a radio station just slightly off frequency.

To distract myself, I let my gaze travel around the room again. The gleam of copper pans, the leaded glass in the windows, the tin punch light fixtures—it was the kind of space that made you pause. That made you feel.

That old itch stirred again. I'd always loved houses—walking through them, stepping into the stories they told. And maybe, just maybe, this was the moment to pivot.

A breath between careers. A chance to exhale the life I'd outgrown and inhale something new.

Becoming a realtor had always been one of those 'maybe someday' ideas I kept tucked away—half-serious, half-dream. But now it felt tangible. My graphic design background wouldn't go to waste—staging, branding, marketing, brochures. I could picture it clearly: walking through homes, listening to what they whispered, helping someone else fall in love.

The idea sat comfortably beside the coffee. Familiar. Possible. Something warm to hold onto. I could almost see it. Not just a new job—A new chapter, a fresh path.

"So," Anna said, interrupting my thoughts, "are you enjoying your new home?"

She said it lightly, but there was a strange weight behind the word *enjoying.* Like it carried a double meaning.

"It's… beautiful," I said carefully. "We fell in love with it the moment we saw it. And it's even prettier now that it's finally ours." I added.

Anna nodded slowly, but something in her expression shifted. Her smile lingered, but her eyes were doing something else—calculating. Searching. Like she was waiting for me to crack.

She watched me the way my mother used to when she knew I was lying. Quiet. Patient. Knowing the truth would spill out eventually.

I turned the tables. "How long have you lived here?"

Anna's face relaxed. "Forty-five years this fall. Moved in just after we got married and raised all five of our kids here —four boys and a girl."

Her voice warmed as she talked about the house, her family, the grandchildren who played in the pond. I had noticed the large pond in the backyard when I'd walked up the drive.

There was a little dock, maybe eight feet long, stretching a bit out over the water, and a small upside-down canoe pulled up on the grass nearby. It looked like the kind of place childhood lived best—muddy, mosquito-bitten, full of belly flops and dares.

I could see it so clearly: balled-up bread pressed onto hooks, kids squealing as fish nibbled too close. Girls running from boys pretending to be monsters, only to get chased off the dock and vanish in a flurry of bubbles and screams. Laughter so pure and bright it rang out like summer lightning.

The vision bloomed, warm and nostalgic—until something caught behind my ribs. A twist.

Just a memory, small and sharp, trying to surface.

I pushed it back down, where it always waited. In that familiar dark corner I'd never fully unpacked. My father's voice echoed faintly—*I'll always be here for you, baby girl*—but I blinked it away.

"So," I said, steering back to the present, "did you know the Millers well?"

Anna shifted in her seat.

"The Millers...?"

"Henry and Sandra Miller," I clarified. "The couple who owned the house before us."

Recognition flickered in her eyes, followed by a quick mask of indifference.

"Oh. Yes. The Millers. Can't say we knew them well. They weren't here long."

"Do you know why they left?" I asked, keeping my tone light.

Anna stood abruptly, lifting the coffee pot. "More?"

I covered my cup with my hand. "I'm good. Otherwise I'll be vibrating until midnight."

She chuckled, but it sounded thinner now. Her shoulders had tensed.

I tried again. "They did a beautiful job on the kitchen renovation. I love all the choices they made—it feels so warm and homey."

Anna didn't answer right away. She ran her finger around the rim of her mug, staring into the dark swirl inside like she might read it.

"They finished that kitchen after they left," she said quietly. "They started it, and something must've changed. A job offer, maybe. They were gone before they could appreciate it."

She finally looked at me. Her smile had disappeared.

"They only lived there for six weeks."

The silence that followed was weighted and strange. Six weeks. Barely enough time to settle in. Barely enough time to hang pictures, let alone plan an exit.

Anna's stare said the conversation was over.

We drifted onto safer ground then—kids, grandkids, hardware stores, recipes. The kind of topics that smooth over awkward beginnings. But this time, it wasn't just polite chatter. Anna had this dry humor that caught me off guard, and before long, we were trading stories like old neighbors.

She scribbled her number on the back of a receipt and handed it over with a smile that didn't feel forced. "Stop by anytime," she said.

We hugged—not politely, but genuinely—and I started the walk home with something lighter in my chest.

Her house was warm, old, honest. The kind of place you leave already missing.

Chapter Six

The nylon walls hummed with the wind. Moonlight bled through the seams of the tent, casting shadows that twitched with every breeze. I was cocooned inside a sleeping bag, buried so deep I couldn't feel my own limbs. Cold gnawed at the edges, biting through the layers like it knew how to find me.

The fire must've died hours ago, but the smell of ash still lingered—wet, acrid, heavy in the air.

Everything was muffled. The quiet was unnatural, like the world was holding its breath. I tried to shift, to pull the zipper down, to move toward air—but the sleeping bag tightened around me. Nylon against skin.

Too close. Too tight.

The scent of smoke was stronger now. Closer. Like the campfire had crept inside.

I couldn't find the opening. My fingers fumbled, clawing, and the more I fought, the more it clung to me. My chest began to rise faster. Too fast. Panic pooled in my throat. I opened my mouth—but the breath wouldn't come. The smoke was thick now—sharp, clinging to the back of my tongue.

There was air above me—I could feel it, sense it—but I couldn't gulp it in. It was hitched, not releasing in the back of my throat. I was gasping—nothing. No air. It was right there—I knew it was—but I... I couldn't. I couldn't breathe. I couldn't—

Everything went gray around the edges. My heart pounded like a drum in water.

And then—Luke's voice, far away. Distant, frantic. Calling my name like he was shouting through the trees.

I woke to Luke's hands prying a pillow from my face and untangling the bed linens from around my legs.

"What the hell happened?" I croaked.

His hands were shaking as he worked to free me from the twisted sheets. "I don't know. You were thrashing in your sleep, like... like you were drowning. The blankets were wrapped around you like a straightjacket. And you were yelling —except it was hard to hear you, because your mouth was closed, and you had this pillow clutched over your head."

He grabbed the pillow and demonstrated — jaw clenched, throat pulsing with a low, desperate, muffled sound. It was eerie, watching him mimic it. Like reliving something that should've stayed buried in my sleep.

I swallowed. "I was dreaming I was camping. Cold. I couldn't breathe. I felt like my sleeping bag was a prison, I couldn't get out. It felt so real—I could even smell the campfire smoke."

Luke pushed himself upright against the headboard, the covers gathered around his waist. "Well, that's just it," he said flatly. "I woke up freezing. The windows were wide open. The room smelled like wet smoke again. Stronger than usual."

My stomach turned.

"And that's not all," he added, rubbing a hand over his face. "I could hear water running. The bathroom faucets were on full blast—tub *and* sink. Water everywhere. Towels on the floor, soaked through.

"I got up to turn off the water and then clean up. And when I came back, the smell was gone—and you were flailing around like you were trying to claw your way out of a casket." He rubbed his hands down his face. "Why would you open the windows in the middle of the night in March?"

I narrowed my eyes. "Why would you think I opened them?"

He stared at me. "Because I didn't. And if I didn't, then who?"

He threw back the covers and stood abruptly. I glanced at the clock. 5:26. Almost time to get up anyway.

His anger didn't feel directed at me, not really. It felt bigger than either of us—aimed at something we couldn't name.

Downstairs, the silence was thick. Luke sat back from the table, elbows on his knees, studying his hands like they might offer answers. I moved through the kitchen automatically—cereal bowls, spoons, bananas, milk. The rhythm of normalcy.

He didn't move to help like he always did. Didn't look up.

My jaw tightened. I slammed his coffee mug down harder than necessary, a bitter slosh soaking into the placemat.

He blinked up at me, startled. "Oh." He reached for the cereal and poured mechanically.

I sat across from him, arms folded, waiting for my turn with the cereal box. The resentment was sharp and rising, I didn't know from where or why, so I forced it back. No point in letting it take over. Not when something worse already had its grip on us.

I tried small talk. Weather. Weekend plans. Anything to drag us back into the shallows.

Eventually, he blinked and said, "Huh?"

"You're not listening," I snapped.

"I'm sorry." He looked up at me, hollow. "I'm just tired."

He went back to watching the spoon disappear into his cereal like he couldn't remember what it was for.

I exhaled hard. "This wouldn't have anything to do with this morning, would it?"

His shoulders sagged. The words came slow.

"I don't know what to make of it anymore. Everything I believe says there's got to be a rational explanation. And maybe there is—if it was just one thing. But it's not. It's everything."

He looked up at me, eyes dark with something I hadn't seen in him before.

"The smells. The windows. The soot. The picture frames. The furniture moving. Now this morning—you almost suffocating in your sleep. It's not random. It feels... deliberate. It's starting to feel … personal. Like something is trying to get our attention. Or force us out."

He hesitated. Then:

"Or worse."

I chilled instantly and stared into my coffee. I had nothing to say. No logic. No comfort. Just a growing sense of dread curling around my spine like a tendril of smoke.

I reached across the table and laid my hand on top of his. His fingers were cold.

He managed a crooked half-smile. It didn't reach his eyes. But I held on anyway—because I needed the reminder that we were still on the same side. And I wasn't ready to risk the one thing that felt like solid ground. And because sometimes, pretending is the only thing that keeps you sitting at the table.

Chapter Seven

I didn't tell Luke, but I was working on a quiet little scheme in the back of my mind. Nothing criminal—just a little social espionage.

Instead of leaving my thank-you note for Shelly in the mailbox, I decided I'd deliver it by hand. Catch her when she was home, flash a smile, and ease my way inside. I was curious if she'd clam up like Anna had when I mentioned the house and the people who used to live there—or if Shelly was more the type to let the gossip tumble out of her if someone was patient enough to listen. I had a hunch she was.

After Luke headed out, I busied myself with the dishes, wiped down the counters, and tossed a load of laundry in the washer. I showered, pulled on jeans, boots, and a cozy sweater layered with a down vest and scarf. The thank-you card was clutched tightly in my bare hand as I walked up the drive.

It was the only other house on this stretch of road—a pale green farmhouse with white trim, tucked quietly among a clutch of trees like it was trying not to be noticed. The crisp

March air bit at my cheeks as I crossed the gravel, arms folded tight across my chest—not just against the cold, but the nerves fluttering under my skin. My heart ticked faster than it should have for a simple neighborly visit.

When I knocked, I heard a muffled, "Just a second!" followed by movement behind the curtains.

She parted the sheer panel on the sidelight, and I gave her a polite, 'caught-you' smile and a small wave. She didn't wave back. I could practically see the inner monologue behind her eyes: How do I get out of this now?

A second later, the door cracked open just wide enough for half of her face and four short, but neatly manicured fingers to appear. Her grip on the edge of the door suggested she was ready to shut it the moment I delivered my thanks and turned to leave.

I launched my plan into action.

"Hi, Shelly," I said quickly, thrusting the card toward her, trying to smooth away the awkwardness. "Thank you for the pie—it was amazing. I didn't have your last name or your exact address, so I thought I'd drop this off in person."

She hesitated a moment, then stepped out from behind the door to take the note. I saw my chance and pushed the idea gently. "Honestly, we've never tasted anything like it. It was so good, I was hoping you'd share your recipe?"

There was a pause, then the door opened wider. The corners of her mouth lifted into something that resembled a smile, though not without effort.

"Well, come on in," she said, stepping back with a flutter of her hand. "I'm so glad you liked it!"

"Oh, I don't want to intrude," I hedged, still half on the porch. "If you're busy—"

"Nonsense." She waved me in. "I'm just watching the Today Show. I love that Hoda Kotb, don't you? Well—" she caught herself and laughed awkwardly. "I DVR it anyway. I can watch later and skip all the fluff. There's only so many times you can watch Al Roker tell people the weather like it's a revelation."

And just like that, she was back to the babbling woman from my doorstep. Familiar. Disarming.

"Coffee?" she offered.

"If it's no trouble," I said, already stepping inside, my cloak-and-dagger intentions already unraveling just a little.

"Not at all. We've got a Keurig. I can whip up a cup of anything in no time." She led me into the kitchen, still talking. "DVRs, Keurigs, texting—I honestly don't know how we lived only a few mere decades ago."

Her kitchen was something else. A portal.

While ours—like Anna's—leaned into the historic, with wide-plank floors and deep sills, Shelly's looked straight out of a 1940s postcard. Hoosier cabinet. A free-standing lower cabinet with porcelain sink and a built-in rinse board. A small bank of white cabinets edged in red. Open shelves. Foam green laminate counters that matched the worn linoleum tiles on the floor. The table was chrome-rimmed, gray Formica with red vinyl chairs like the ones from an old diner. It was charming, retro, and completely unexpected.

She noticed me taking it in. "Believe it or not, I picked all of this out on purpose," she said, eyes searching mine for judgment. "My grandmother raised me since I was fourteen in a kitchen just like this. I wanted it to feel like that again— warm bread, pies cooling, lemonade in a Mason jar... all that good stuff."

"I get it," I said sincerely. "My grandma's house was like that too. Smelled like cornbread and Jergens lotion." I grinned, and so did she. "I love that you stuck to your style. It's refreshing."

As she rattled off coffee options, I nodded, and she popped a pod into the machine. While it sputtered to life, she retrieved a box of recipe cards from the Hoosier cabinet and flipped through them. She pulled out two blue index cards, one blank, and hunted for a pen.

The aroma of brewed coffee filled the room. She set a cup in front of me. "Milk and sugar?"

I shook my head. "No thanks," and followed her to the table. She set her mug down, slid into the seat across from me, and started writing.

I eased into it. "So… are you from around here?"

She glanced up briefly, pen poised. "Not far. Grew up in town. My parents ran a little hotel there, actually. We lived on the bottom floor until…" She trailed off. Her face shifted—shadowed, distant—before she pasted on the semblance of a smile. "… until they died. I was fourteen. That's when my grandmother took me in. After they passed, my grandmother was amazing and stepped up." She paused, "Hence the kitchen."

She returned to writing, but I wasn't letting go.

"Oh… gosh, I'm so sorry," I said, the words slipping out instinctively. "That must've been awful."

She gave a soft, noncommittal shrug without looking up.

"Were you an only child?" I asked gently.

"Mm-hmm."

"If it's okay to ask… how did they die?"

Even as I said it, guilt surged. I hadn't meant to press. But something about the way she'd told the story—it felt like a door cracking open. I didn't want to walk past it.

Her pen slowed. She finished a word, placed the pen down, and looked up—eyes wet, but steady. "Fire," she said softly.

A pause.

"I wasn't there. I'd gone to the fair with a friend and begged to stay over at her house. They almost didn't let me. I had to promise I'd be up early, clean, ready for church. That was a non-negotiable. We were Mennonite." She gave a tiny shrug, as if that explained everything.

She rose to get a tissue, dabbed first at her eyes, then her nose, then sat again.

"The fire started just before midnight. Someone dropped a cigarette in their room. My parents tried to make sure everyone else got out. They didn't."

She blew her nose. The story was compact, precise, practiced. Years of repetition had made it tidy. Too tidy for all the emotion that must be attached to it.

"I was supposed to be there," she added quietly.

I knew that guilt. I recognized its weight immediately— how it settled in the tiny corners of your days and made a home there. It didn't scream. It didn't even speak most of the time. It just existed—always present, always pressing. You went on living around it, adjusting to it, the way you'd learn to walk with a limp. And sometimes, when you forgot it was there, it shifted just enough to remind you: you hadn't let go. Not really.

"I get it," I said.

She tilted her head, searching my face.

"I lost my dad when I was seven," I continued. "We were supposed to go fishing together. I found him… later. In the lake. I always thought if I'd been there sooner, or if I was stronger, maybe—"

She reached across the table, laid her hand over mine.

"I'm so sorry," she said, voice low.

Shame flooded me. I'd come here with an agenda. A question hidden behind a perfunctorily penned thank you note and polite conversation. But somehow, in the space of a few shared memories, we weren't strangers anymore. The air between us felt warmer now, like something had quietly shifted. I hadn't come looking for connection—but here it was anyway.

"I didn't mean to just dump all that. It's just ... it's been ages, but it all still feels so fresh. I've not met anyone in a long time that had a similar circumstance. You know, not just losing a parent, but having that guilt," I clarified. "As an adult, I don't think I've ever spoken about this. I hear the self-pity rearing its ugly head again, and I hate the sound of it."

"Well, then. You obviously need to get it out." Shelly was not letting me off the hook.

So I continued, "My mom kind of... disappeared for a while. Not literally. She was there, but not there. I looked after my little sister the best I could. Then overnight, it seemed, she —my mother—she re-emerged—only it wasn't to be a mother. She was heading to the bar, dressed up, too much makeup, laughing too loud, a martini always in hand as the final accessory. There were babysitters and whispers and other neighborhood moms who knew too much."

I shook my head, clearing the fog.

"She was masking her pain, I know that now. But back then, it just felt like we didn't matter anymore."

Shelly watched me. There was no pity in her eyes—just understanding.

"You're not done," she said.

I smiled. Busted.

"No," I admitted. "There's more. Some guy started coming around. Polyester suit. Creepy mustache. Leisure Suit Larry vibes. He brought gifts. Too many gifts. My sister and I had every My Little Pony and Barbie accessory known to man. We were the envy of every girl in the neighborhood for that, so it was exciting at first. But I knew even then—he wasn't buying us toys. He was buying our silence. A way to make us blend into the wallpaper. Seen and not heard."

"And it's not that I begrudged my mother her happiness," I went on. "At least I didn't think I did. He wasn't

114

a bad man. He just had the undeniable misfortune of being, 'not my dad.' But he wasn't even a close second. My dad, who had always been strong and self-assured and smart and fun and a good, attentive dad, was being replaced by this... this sleazy used-car salesman in a polyester suit."

The last part came out in a rush—like a gasp I didn't know I'd been holding for years, a pressure valve I hadn't realized was sealed shut.

I panicked then, and with a hand half-clamped over my mouth, mumbled, "Your husband isn't a used car salesman, I hope. 'Cause if so, I think I just managed to really stick my foot in it."

I looked at her sheepishly.

She laughed easily. "No worries there. My husband is an actuary. Definitely not a used car salesman! But he does like his polyester." She looked up at me with a smirk, then a wink.

We both laughed comfortably. I was swiftly changing my mind about this neighbor.

Then her voice shifted again, softer now. "You know…
for a long time, I carried it too. The guilt. Not being there. Not
saying goodbye. Wondering what would've happened if I'd
stayed home that night."

She looked at me—not with pity, not with judgment.
Just clarity.

"But that thinking—it's a trap. You get stuck in that
loop long enough, it starts to feel like purpose. Like
punishment you chose."

She gave a small, almost invisible shrug. "Eventually, I
had to let the ghosts be… just ghosts. Memories, not weights.

"I still miss them," she said simply. "But I stopped
asking why. There's no good answer to that question."

She went quiet then, fingertips grazing a wrinkle in her
napkin.

And I…I wasn't sure what I expected her to say—that
she still had nightmares, maybe. That she sometimes forgot
how to breathe on anniversaries. But she didn't. And I

wondered how she'd made her peace with the unfairness of it all, while I still felt left with the weight of what could've been.

After a moment, she added, almost offhandedly, "He actually used to be a volunteer fireman."

There was a shift in her posture, subtle but telling—she brushed at the table like there was a crumb, though there wasn't. Her gaze slid toward the window, distant.

"That's how we met," she continued, more gently now. "He was on duty the night the hotel burned down."

Her voice softened further. "It was one of his first calls —he was just twenty then, still new enough that it all hit him hard. He came to the funeral. I barely remembered it, honestly. But afterward, he started stopping by my grandmother's place every so often. Just to see how I was doing. No pressure, just kindness."

She smiled to herself, a little wistfully. "I think he could see I was carrying too much. And maybe I leaned on him more than I meant to. I didn't have anyone else who really saw me, you know? Not like that."

Then she looked back at me, her voice gaining strength. "But it wasn't until years later—when I was grown—that we... well, things shifted. It just happened gradually. A friendship that turned into something more."

Her fingers played with the edge of her napkin now, but it didn't seem like embarrassment. More like... hesitation. She was holding a secret that wasn't quite ready to surface. Something she wasn't quite ready to tell me.

Then, softly, "But this is your story."

I shook my head. "Feels like we've carried different versions of the same weight. I'm really glad you told me your story. And thank you for letting me share mine."

Her answer was only a small smile, but something in it felt like grace.

Chapter Eight

It was funny, the things you forgot when you moved. Not that I'd done it that many times, but each time, I found myself surprised by what resurfaced—bits of life boxed away, carted from house to house, quietly biding their time until they emerged again like forgotten relics.

Luke was at work, so I headed to the back guest room, and dug a utility knife from my back pocket with something close to Christmas-morning anticipation and sliced open the next box. A puff of stale air escaped as I peeled the flaps back. I reached inside and pulled free a wad of crumpled paper— Luke's old sports trophies. As I unwrapped the first one, my skin prickled. A tight shimmer rolled up the side of my face and down my neck, and I froze mid-motion.

I didn't move. My body went still—listening. The air had shifted. Denser, like something was occupying the space just behind me.

Then—barely there—a whisper traced the back of my neck. Cold. Intentional.

An unintentional shiver ran up my back. Then—like the weight of a palm settling gently on my shoulder—something touched me. Cold, yet familiar. And wrong.

I turned my head slowly, afraid I already knew what I'd find. But there was no one, and nothing, there.

Still, the feeling stuck. Heavy. Watchful.

Nope. Not doing this again today.

I stood up abruptly, placed the trophy back into its nest of paper, and made a beeline for my iPod and speaker. Music. I needed sound. Something normal. Something to fill the space. I plugged in the speaker, dropped it unceremoniously on the floor, and cranked the volume. Too high—but I didn't care. I needed to drown out the nerves clawing up the back of my neck.

Just my imagination. That's all. New house, unfamiliar shadows, no cozy clutter to dull all the corners yet. My psyche was having a field day. Freud would've had a blast with me.

Jann Arden's voice seeped into the room, mournful and smoky, singing about living under some woman named June. I nodded to no one, pushed up the sleeves of my sweatshirt, and got back to it. I dusted the top of the waist-high bookshelf, then started arranging Luke's trophies and mementos one by one, playing curator.

Glass ball in hand—a tennis trophy—I paused to consider spacing, and that's when I saw it.

The silver football trophy on the top shelf.

It moved.

It scooted. Slowly, erratically, like it was being dragged by a hand I couldn't see. It jerked its way to the edge of the shelf and dropped, then landed at my feet with a metallic thunk. The base cracked free and the miniature football spun away, wobbling a few feet before coming to a stop.

I shrieked. Loud. Unfiltered.

Still clutching the glass trophy like a weapon, I bolted. Down the stairs, through the kitchen, and out the back screen door. I could still hear the threads of the music from upstairs. My lungs burned. My heart was a drumline.

Outside, in the daylight, everything felt absurd. My bare feet on the cool porch planks. The scent of newly growing grass and earth. The soundtrack of birds and wind. Had I imagined it?

I started to breathe again.

Then, without knowing why, I suddenly turned back toward the house.

And there he was.

A man. Inside my kitchen. Standing by the island. Silent. Watching.

He didn't move. His hands hung loosely at his sides. Dark hair. Dark eyes. His gaze locked with mine through the storm door, and something cold and ancient twisted in my gut.

I couldn't breathe. Couldn't move. My hand rose instinctively to my mouth, as if to cork the scream rising in my throat.

And then—he shimmered. Like heat on pavement.

And vanished.

I stared. At the place he'd been. At the clean, empty space that should've felt like relief, but didn't.

I couldn't go back inside. Not yet. Not for my phone. Not for my keys. So I ran. Not caring what I looked like, or what any of the neighbors might think. Not even caring that I was leaving my house completely unlocked. I sprinted down the long gravel drive, not even feeling the sharp stones tearing into the tender soles of my feet, and turned toward Anna's.

My lungs were aching by the time I reached her door. I knocked harder than I meant to, pausing only long enough to notice the brass "No Solicitors" sign. I winced. Did neighborly panic count as solicitation?

Too late. Anna appeared, apron and all, as if summoned by script.

And the moment she opened the door, I knew. She'd been expecting this.

"Hi, Anna," I managed, winded and disheveled. I was covered in dust and wearing an old paint-spattered WVU sweatshirt, hair glued to my forehead in sweaty strands, and bare dirty feet, "Can I come in?"

"Of course," she said, stepping aside with a gentle sweep of her hand. But her eyes held something behind the welcome—recognition, maybe. Or resignation.

We were still in the hallway when I blurted it all out. Everything. The boxes. The movement. The man. My panic. The running. I couldn't stop once I started. My voice shook. My hands trembled.

She listened in silence. When I finally ran out of breath, the house fell quiet. It was only then I had realized how long and how loud I'd been speaking.

Anna let out a long, slow sigh and gently took my hand.

"Come have a cup of coffee, dear one."

It sounded like an offer, but it settled in the air like a command—quiet, certain, and not really up for debate. She'd been ready for this chapter to begin.

She poured my coffee just the way I like it—without asking. She remembered. And something about that small, unspoken care grounded me.

Once we were seated at the table, steam rising between us, she said, "I've been wondering when you were going to come back."

There was something in her voice. Regret. Sorrow. Maybe both.

"I figured you were," I said with a half-smile.

That earned the smallest upturn of her lips.

I leapt right on it. "What can you tell me about my house. What you've heard?" I asked. "Or seen. Or know."

She wrapped her hands around her mug. "Well," she said quietly. "I suppose I should start at the beginning."

Anna began to recount her visits with Sandra Miller, the woman who had lived in the house before us.

"They were a nice couple, with three children—two boys and a girl. The oldest boy was twelve, and the youngest two, a boy and a girl, were twins, both eight." I nodded. Things I already knew.

"I didn't know them very well," she went on. "They really weren't here very long at all. And they were quiet. They were actually the first family to live in that house for a long, long time." Anna looked down into her coffee cup and paused.

"Sandra brought the kids down here not long after they moved in. They'd smelled smoke in the house and couldn't find the source. She was worried. Wanted to be sure the kids were safe. So she brought them here, introduced herself, and asked for my help."

I kept quiet, hoping more would spill out if I didn't interrupt.

"After that first visit, I begged her to bring them again. I loved having them here. Sweet kids. I made chicken nuggets and cookies and lemonade. They'd fish in the pond..."

Yeah, yeah, I thought. So what. Get to the good stuff.

"They got comfortable here," Anna continued. "And when things really started going haywire in the house, they spent more and more time with me."

She leaned forward slightly, her voice softening. "The twins were intuitive. They seemed to understand something wasn't right. They told me, 'Mrs. Anna'—that's what they called me—'there's another man in our house. He makes it smell weird and he moves our stuff around.'" She looked at me meaningfully, letting the words sink in. A pattern, repeating itself.

"I asked Sandra about it once, when she came to pick them up, while the kids were still outside playing. She was hesitant at first, but eventually, she shared a few of the same things you just did."

I studied her face. She wasn't telling me everything. I could feel it.

Anna's hands trembled. She avoided my eyes.

"They left when he tried to kill the oldest boy," she said, her voice barely more than a whisper. I had to watch her lips to understand the words.

"What do you mean 'he tried to kill the oldest boy?'" I asked, alarmed. "When *who* tried to kill the oldest boy? The father? Or the... the..." What was I even supposed to call it?

"The ghost," she hissed. Her voice held a bitterness that startled me.

I simply nodded.

"Yes. Whatever was living in that house with them. They packed up in the middle of the night and never came back. Sandra stopped by once to thank me for caring for the kids. She said something had tried to suffocate Alex in the middle of the night. That they couldn't stay any longer. That was it."

She seemed finished, but I wasn't ready to let it go.

"That's all she said?" I pressed, my tone sharper than I intended. Heat rushed to my ears. "That he'd been suffocated, but she didn't say by what? And she never came back? After all you did for those kids. That doesn't make sense. And what about the people before them? You've lived here forever—you must remember others."

I was practically interrogating her, but I didn't care. I lived in that house. I needed answers, and she clearly had them. Maybe not all, but more than I had right now.

Anna shifted in her seat, rubbed her face with both hands, then slumped back and let her hands fall into her lap. She shook her head and groaned.

"Of course I remember." She paused, and for a moment I thought that was all she'd say. But then, almost wistfully, she added, "Jacquelyn and Ryan. They were such a sweet young couple. So in love. It was heartbreaking, how they died. So young. So horrifically."

Wait. What?

"What do you mean, 'taken so young and horrifically?'" I interrupted. "What happened to them?"

Anna squinted and gazed out the kitchen window toward the street, as if she could see the past unfolding again before her.

"No one knows how she got out of the house that night. Or why he didn't. It's one of those things that haunts you," Anna said quietly. "No pun intended," she looked at me sheepishly, realizing her faux pas. "I didn't hear anything—no screams, no glass breaking, nothing—until the emergency vehicles arrived. The road filled up fast. Four fire trucks. Two ambulances. More state police cars than I'd ever seen. Parked all the way from their house to nearly ours."

She paused, her lips pressing into a thin line before continuing.

"I went outside, of course. Everyone on the block did. But no one knew what was going on yet. It was dark, the whole sky lit orange from the flames. And then—" she swallowed hard, her voice catching. "Then I saw them covering something on the side of the road. At first, I didn't know what to think."

She closed her eyes briefly.

"It was her. Jacquelyn. She'd made it out and tried to flag down help. A tractor-trailer was coming down the hill. The driver saw the smoke, but not her. Not until it was too late."

A sick heaviness settled into my stomach.

Anna's voice was quieter now, thin and shaky. "I didn't understand everything that had happened until the next morning, when it was all over the news. The fire. The crash. The couple. That poor girl dying in the street while he died in the house. The pieces didn't come together until later—but I was there. I had seen enough."

I must've looked like I'd been hit by a two-by-four.

Anna's face crumpled. "Oh, sweetheart," she said gently. "No one told you they both died at your house, did they?"

I closed my eyes and gave the faintest shake of my head. A wave of heat and nausea crashed through me, and I heard the dull roar of the ocean in my ears. I held up a hand to stop her, just until I could steady myself.

When I could finally speak, I rasped, "So she got out... but he didn't?" My voice cracked. "Why didn't he run too?"

I sat upright, rigid in my chair, needing to know the truth.

"No one knows, dear," Anna said quickly, shaking her head.

"Wow." I collapsed back into my seat. "Wow, wow, wow. I had no idea. That's so sad." It was the only coherent thought I could manage.

Everything inside me was spinning.

"So while he was taking his last breath, he had no idea she was taking hers too," I murmured. The thought twisted in my chest.

Anna nodded and took a sip of coffee. Her face had gone pale, her breathing shallow and fast.

"Oh, Anna. I'm so sorry. I didn't mean to upset you. Are you alright? Do you want some water?"

I teetered between feeling entitled to answers and guilty for making this sweet woman relive something so painful.

She waved me off. "It's okay. I just haven't thought about this in years. But I think you need to know." I nodded, letting the silence stretch before asking the next question.

"Did they have children?"

Anna exhaled slowly. "No, honey. Praise the Good Lord," she said, though her voice was thick with sorrow. "They wanted them. But it never happened. There was a rumor... that she may have been pregnant when she died. But it was just a rumor. No one ever confirmed it. Not that I heard, anyway..."

I let the weight of it settle over me. A fresh grief bloomed in my chest for a couple I'd never known but somehow felt connected to. Luke and I were also childless, not entirely by choice, and very much in love. I wondered if they had fought the same silent battles we had—the kind no one talks about at parties or family picnics. In that moment, I felt an aching kinship to the woman whose home I now lived in.

Anna interrupted my thoughts. "You know who you should talk to? Your neighbor to the west. Her name is Shelly."

I straightened at the sound of her name.

"Shelly? Why?"

"She married a fireman. He was on the scene that morning." I gaped open-mouthed at Anna.

Well. That explained a lot, didn't it?

Anna and I sat in silence for a long moment, letting the weight of it all settle between us like a storm cloud that had finally stopped rumbling but refused to pass. I could still hear the faint whoosh of blood in my ears, and the idea of walking back into that house—*our* house—suddenly felt impossible.

Anna must have sensed it. "I'm getting some rolls ready for dinner tonight," she said softly, pushing herself up from the table with a slight wince. "You stay a minute. Help me punch down some dough."

I welcomed the task. The warmth of the kitchen, the simple motion of kneading and shaping the rolls—it grounded me. I found rhythm in it. Once that was done, Anna handed me a paring knife and slid a cutting board of vegetables in front of me, and we worked together in quiet companionship. Before I headed home, she handed me a pair of old clogs to slip on—my raw feet screaming at the notion of walking home barefoot— and told me to keep them until next time.

When I finally left, dusk had settled in. The air was cooler, the sky bruised with purples and grays. Luke pulled into the driveway just as I reached the porch, and I raised a hand in greeting, trying to appear more composed than I felt.

Later, across the dinner table, I told Luke everything.

The cold rush that pinned me in place. The crash of the falling trophy. The apparition in the kitchen. And finally, Anna's quiet, devastating admission: *Two people died in this house.*

I spoke like someone reciting a confession—soft, careful, each detail unfolding with the weight of something sacred yet dangerous.

When I finished, I looked at him.

He sat frozen, fork suspended in the air, his knuckles white against the handle.

"What do you make of all that?" I asked, my voice barely above a whisper. I was still shaking inside.

Luke set his fork down slowly, like he was afraid of making a sudden move that might break the spell. He ran a hand through his hair, then let it fall into his lap. "Jesus, Liz." His voice was raw. "You *saw* him?"

I nodded.

"In the kitchen. Plain as day. And then he just shimmered into nothingness."

He stared at me, like he was trying to reconcile the woman he knew with the words coming out of my mouth.

"And you're sure it wasn't just—" he stopped himself. "No. Never mind. I know you. You wouldn't just... make this up."

"I wish I had."

Silence bloomed between us, thick and pulsing. I could see the gears turning in his head, but this wasn't a spreadsheet he could balance. This wasn't his world. Luke dealt in absolutes—spreadsheets, audits, clean numbers that always added up. He was an accountant by degree, a controller for a multinational firm by recent promotion. His job was to make sure everything balanced. Every problem had a formula. Every answer had a logic trail. But this? This was messy. This was 1 + 1 equaling something much stranger than 2. I saw the struggle on his face, the edges of irritability that came from not being able to fix something, not even with the sharpest pencil or the fattest eraser. This was *our house. Our everything.*

His eyes flicked toward the ceiling, like he expected the answer to be up there.

"They both died here?" he repeated.

"Anna said the man died in the fire. His wife made it out, but got run over by a semi on the road. So... not technically *in* the house, but—close enough."

Luke pushed his plate away, appetite gone. "We bought a murder house."

"It wasn't a murder."

"You think that matters?" His voice cracked, and I flinched. "A haunted house, then. Liz, we sank every cent we had into this place. You left your job. We uprooted our lives. We came here to *start over.* Not to play ghost hunters!"

"I'm not playing anything," I said, trying not to raise my voice. "This happened. To *me.* And you don't get to shut it down just because it doesn't fit in your nice little ledger." That last part came out so much harsher than I planned.

He stood abruptly, scraping the chair back against the hardwood. He paced, hands on his hips, breath shallow.

"I don't know what to do with this," he said finally. "I don't know how to protect you. Or even understand what the hell is going on. You're telling me this house is haunted— *actually haunted*—and I'm supposed to do what? How do I protect you? How do I protect us? How do I protect our investment??"

"I don't know. I really don't."

He stopped pacing and looked at me. All the fight drained out of him, replaced by a kind of scared honesty I wasn't used to seeing in him. "Are we safe here, Liz?"

The question hollowed me out.

"I don't know," I whispered.

And that was the worst part.

Chapter Nine

For reasons I couldn't quite explain, I felt more grounded in the kitchen. Not safe, but *less threatened*. Maybe it was the back door just a few feet away—my straight shot out if anything shifted. The echoes of that long, aching conversation with Anna were still murmuring through me. Her voice. Her grief. The weight of everything she'd said. I couldn't be left alone in the house with that.

Upstairs, I felt boxed in. The hallway felt tighter than usual, like the walls had drawn a slow breath and held it. I definitely didn't want to be alone up there. The kitchen had windows. Light. The distant sound of birds. And that would have to be enough for today.

I opened my browser and started with a broad search: *signs of a haunting*. Then I narrowed the scope—names, events, addresses, fires. I scoured old newspaper archives, local blogs, crime forums. But most of what I found was either sensationalist junk or unrelated. The pages stretched on endlessly, but the answers did not.

By the time I poured my second cup of coffee, a chill had crept into the air. I headed upstairs for a sweater.

As I crossed the living room, something snagged my attention—a floorboard, just in front of the built-in bookcase. It sat just slightly higher than the others. Not enough to trip over. Just enough to whisper *notice me*.

I walked over and stepped on it gently. It shifted.

Curious, I pressed my weight on one end and watched the other edge rise. Holding my balance, I crouched down, wedged my fingers beneath it, and pried it loose.

I froze.

Beneath the lifted board was a narrow hollow, quiet and undisturbed. Inside lay a bundle of yellowed envelopes, bound with brittle, fraying twine; beside them, a thick leather-bound book, its faded gold title just barely legible—**Mother Goose's Melodies**—its spine cracked and softened by time; and a small wooden box, dark and dusty with age.

I stared down at the items, unwilling to touch them yet. I could've just reached in and taken them—lifted them out like any other old forgotten thing—but something held me in place.

It didn't feel like I was opening a hiding place. It felt like I was breaking a seal.

This wasn't just a loose floorboard. It was an offering. A moment. A door creaked open to something older, deeper— maybe even sacred.

Something in me whispered that this wasn't an accident. That what lay beneath the floor hadn't simply been left behind—it had been *left for me to find.* For now. For this exact moment.

And I didn't know whether to feel chosen... or cursed.

It didn't feel like I'd discovered something.

It felt like something had been *waiting* for me to look.

I crouched there for what felt like an eternity, breath shallow, heart pounding.

Then, finally—curiosity won.

With one swift motion, I scooped up the bundle and the box, clutching them to my chest as I backed away toward the kitchen. I needed light. I needed coffee. I needed to be near the door.

I set the envelopes gently on the table, untied the brittle twine, and spread them into a neat stack. The box, I left closed for now. The sweater I'd gone upstairs for was completely forgotten.

A half hour later, I'd gone through half a box of tissues and felt like I'd just watched the final scene of a devastating romantic film—the kind where no one gets their happy ending.

The letters were beautiful. Wrenching. Filled with longing and weariness and love that felt too big for the world they lived in. Most were from her to him, which told me he had been the one to hide them. But there were a few cards from him, too—store-bought, but carefully chosen and filled with writing as tender as any poem.

I read them in chronological order, from oldest to newest, bottom of the pile to top. When I finished, I re-stacked them carefully and retied the twine with the reverence that that kind of love deserved.

Next, the Mother Goose book.

I opened it carefully, the pages brittle, edges feathered from years of turning. One by one, I read through the nursery rhymes, even though I already knew every single word by heart, each one unlocking a long-closed door in my memory.

The last time I'd heard them, I'd been curled up in my father's lap, tucked into the crook of his arm in the old chair by the fire. He used to read them to me every night before bed— those, part of only a few favorite stories I made him read again and again.

Funny. I hadn't thought of them in years. Not until now.

Finally, I turned my attention to the box.

It was mahogany, plain, with a small, simple lock on the front. I pulled it toward me and examined the keyhole. No way I was forcing it open. That didn't feel right. I wasn't meant to break into this box.

I picked up the letters and the book and returned them to their hiding place beneath the floorboards, placing them gently as though tucking them into bed. I laid then on my stomach and felt around the space with my fingertips, but found only dust and bits of fuzz. No key.

I rolled onto my back and stared at the ceiling, frustrated and buzzing with the sense that this wasn't random. I was meant to find those letters today. I was meant to find *this* box. And so I was also meant to open it—but not by force.

So I got up.

I started opening every drawer and cupboard in the built-in bookshelf, methodically working through them one by one. Dust. An old button. A stray marble. More dust.

Then, in the fourth drawer—there it was. Small. Brass. Hidden near the back like it had been waiting for someone patient enough to look.

I plucked it from its hiding place and let it settle in my palm, cool and dense. I turned it over slowly, and the metal felt heavier than it should have—like it carried with it the mystery in the box.

I didn't rush. I walked slowly back to the kitchen, the key pressed tight in my fist.

And I wondered: What was I about to unlock?

I held the key and stared at the box for a long time before I could move. It seemed to pulse with whispered memories and secrets of its own. Like it knew it had just completely rearranged the shape of my morning.

I slid the key into the lock. It turned smoothly.

The lid creaked open, and what lay inside was quiet. Intimate. Unmistakably private.

On top was a stack of photographs, worn soft and curled at the corners. I lifted them carefully, one by one.

The first was of the house—*our* house—but not quite. It had been taken from the edge of the driveway in late summer; you could tell by the gold of the light, the long grass, the laundry line swaying gently in the background. But the addition wasn't there. The part of the house that was now the new kitchen and master suite—the part that had been under construction when the fire broke out—was missing. Just sky and yard where walls now stood. The house looked smaller. Simpler. Lighter, somehow. Before.

The next showed a woman seated on the porch steps, barefoot, a book in her lap and a faraway smile on her lips. The photo wasn't posed. It was a moment caught mid-thought, her face in profile, her chin tilted slightly upward, eyes closed. I paused for a second and marveled at how similar our features were. Her dress was wrinkled like she'd been sitting there for hours. A strand of hair had escaped her dark braid. She looked —content. The kind of content that comes from knowing you're well-loved.

The next photo had the same woman, this time wrapped in the arms of a man standing behind her. He was leaning in, kissing her cheek, her hair, long and loose around her shoulders, and she was laughing, but not looking at the camera. They didn't even seem to know it had been taken. It was all light and motion and closeness. A quiet ache bloomed in my chest at the simple beauty of it.

I kept turning over photos. Four. Five. Six. A whole life, flickering in still photographs — Dancing in the kitchen.

146

Sitting on the hood of a car. Her hand on his chest, his fingers tangled in hers.

And then the last one. I started to feel lightheaded.

For the first time, in that particular photo, I could take in the whole of her. Long, dark hair falling in loose waves over her shoulders. Green eyes set in a delicate, heart-shaped face.

I staggered back a step. My stomach dropped, as if the floor had tilted beneath me.

Oh God.

It was like looking into a mirror.

My breath caught in my throat. The resemblance was startling. Same cheekbones. Same eyes. Same tilt of the chin. A surreal, uncanny doubling—like someone had peeled me from my own skin and pressed me into the past. She was taller, more willowy than me, but the echo was unmistakable. And deeply unsettling.

She was breathtaking. Not in a showy way—something quieter. Serene. But it was the glow she carried that held me. A kind of contentment I couldn't ever remember feeling. Peace, not posed.

She stood before a mirror, one hand resting gently on the slight swell of her belly.

She was with child.

The thought hit like a slap. *And baby makes three…*

I sank onto the edge of the stool, gripping the photo with both hands. My fingertips tingled. Somewhere in the back of my mind, a voice whispered: *No wonder Anna looked at you like that.*

My stomach flipped. A cold sweat prickled underneath my hair.

And then—

A deep, bone-vibrating thud shook the floor beneath me. The drawer to my left jerked open with a metallic shriek, slamming shut again just as fast. Chairs scraped violently against the tile, moving on their own as if shoved by invisible hands.

The photos trembled in my grip. One tore free—*that photo*—and spiraled through the air before slapping against a cabinet and sliding to the floor, face-up.

I flinched, instinctively curling over the rest of them like I could shield them—or myself—from whatever storm I'd just unleashed.

"I'm sorry," I whispered, my voice shaking and barely audible over the pounding of my own heart. "I thought you *wanted* me to find these."

For one terrible moment, it felt like the whole kitchen might come apart at the seams — cabinets banging open and closed, the overhead light swaying dangerously.

And then — just as suddenly — it stopped.

The house sagged into a heavy, aching stillness. The only sound left was the sharp, ragged sound of my breathing.

I stayed there a long moment, crouched low, clutching the photos tight against my chest.

Whoever — whatever — had stirred the house into that storm...

I stayed frozen, the photos clutched to my chest.

"I didn't mean any harm," I said softly into the silence. "I just … I just want to understand."

The words felt strange in my mouth, I didn't know who or what I was speaking to.

I waited — heart thudding — for some sign, some shift in the heavy air.

None came. Only that weighted, aching quiet.

Carefully, I set the photos aside and tentatively looked back into the box.

Beneath the photos, folded in a small square of worn cotton—faded tight florals printed across fabric that looked like it had once been chosen with care—was a single sprig of forget-me-nots—pressed flat, preserved carefully. Each little bloom was barely the size of my fingernail—fragile, blue, with a pin-sized dot of golden light at its core. A gold chain lay tangled beside it, with a beautiful gold locket on the end, a small flower etched in it along the lower left arc of the piece. It was nearly identical to the forget-me-nots — five petals, a pinprick hollow at its center — delicate and small. I held my breath as I snapped open the locket. It was strangely empty, though—two smooth gold frames, not just untouched, but aching with the shape of what might have been.

Resting in the corner of the box, was a small, worn silver button etched with a curling pattern I couldn't quite decipher. Ivy, maybe? I turned it over in my hand several times before replacing it.

The box itself smelled faintly of earth and old perfume. And last, at the very bottom, folded with care, was a single torn sheet of paper.

The handwriting was strong and looping. And what was written was lightly poetic.
Incredibly raw.

"There is no world where I forget you. If I am scattered, I will gather myself back to your side. You are my one and only direction. My true north. I'll always be here for you."

My breath caught in my throat and I heard my father's voice. *I'll always be here for you.* I knew that was a common phrase, but in the moment I heard him clear as day. I felt it clanging in my body, like the clarity of a church bell in winter air—undeniable and sharp.

There was no name on the note. No signature. Just the echo of something fierce and unfinished. And it pulsed in me. It echoed with a remembrance, with a familiarity I held onto with all my might.

I read it again. And again.

I didn't know what any of it meant. Didn't know why exactly I was led to that loose floorboard. But I could feel it. A love so large it had nowhere left to go.

I had the sense that I wasn't just holding their tragic story.

I was holding the part they'd left behind.

It was almost midnight when I finally sat down with Luke.

The box was on the coffee table between us. I'd taken a shower. Poured wine. Braced myself. But nothing made it easier.

"I found this earlier today," I said quietly. "Under the floorboards."

Luke gave a cautious nod but said nothing.

I lifted out the stack of photographs, fingers trembling slightly, and passed them to him.

"They're old. From before the fire. From when they lived there."

He took the top one—a picture of the house before the addition—and studied it. Then another. A woman on the porch. The two of them wrapped in each other's arms. Quiet moments, real ones. Something flickered in his eyes.

And then he got to *that* photo. The one of her standing in front of a mirror, hand resting on the slight curve of her belly. Peaceful. Glowing. Her green eyes lifted toward the lens, soft and full of unspoken joy.

His whole body went still.

153

Luke's breath caught. He looked at me, then back at the picture, then back again.

"Is this supposed to be funny?" he asked. His voice was flat, but sharp around the edges.

I blinked. "What?"

"This." He held the photo up, shaking it once. "What the hell is this, Liz? Is this some kind of joke?"

My chest tightened. "Luke, no. I just found it. I'm not —"

"Jesus." He pushed back on the couch, standing now, staring down at the photo like it might catch fire in his hand. "It's you. It *is* you. Liz, that's you in this picture."

"It's not," I said, too fast.

He looked at me like he didn't believe me. Like he didn't know me.

"It's not," I repeated. "It's her. Jacquelyn. I didn't— until I saw that one, I didn't know how much we… that I look like her."

Luke ran a hand through his hair, pacing now. "That's not just a resemblance. That's *you*. How can that be?"

"I don't know. Maybe it's coincidence. Or maybe it's why everything's been so... off."

He stopped pacing. "You think the house is haunted because you look like her?"

I nodded. "Maybe he thinks I *am* her."

Luke went quiet. He didn't sit back down.

"I don't want this in the house," he said finally, his voice low. "Burn it. Or bury it. Just—get rid of it."

I didn't answer. I couldn't. Because as shaken as he was...

I wasn't ready to let it go.

Chapter Ten

I was wandering barefoot through unfamiliar woods. The pine needles had formed a soft blanket over the forest floor. It felt cool and spongy under my feet. Once in a while an errant needle pricked the sole of my foot. I stooped down, and easily pulled it out before moving on.

I was searching.

For what, I didn't know.

Something shimmered at the edge of my awareness—slipping just out of reach every time I tried to focus. But I kept moving forward. I somehow knew the direction, the way a body knows the shape of a familiar dream. I'd been here before. I was sure of it.

Though the woods were dark, the moonlight filtered down through the trees in broken ribbons, slicing through the mist and illuminating patches of my path in silver. I gathered the sides of my nightgown in my hands, lifting the damp hem away from the dew-soaked ground. Morning was coming. I couldn't see the sun yet, but I felt its weight rising beneath the earth.

The mist thickened. It curled upward from the ground and wrapped around me, whirling in lazy spirals, cool and weightless It swirled around me, enveloping me in its gossamer arms.

Behind me, a branch snapped.

I froze mid-stride, my foot hovering above the ground, and turned my head slowly toward the sound.

The woods answered with silence.

Then—panting. Shallow, frantic. As if someone nearby had been running too long and could no longer catch their breath.

The calm broke like glass inside me. My limbs snapped into motion. I ran.

I couldn't hear footsteps, but I felt them—felt the weight of someone closing in. Not beside me. Behind me. Pressing closer with every stride. The pounding of my heart wasn't just in my chest anymore—it was in the ground, the air, the trees.

My breath came in ragged, tearing gasps. The mist clung to my skin like cobwebs. The forest around me began to shift—branches leaning in, roots reaching just enough to catch my feet. I stumbled over something unseen.

When I regained my balance, I turned. Ready to face whatever chased me.

But before I could see—
I was shoved backward, into the brush.
A weight crashed against me.
An invisible hand over my mouth.
An unseen body pinning me still.
I couldn't scream.

The acrid sting of smoke flooded my nose and clawed down my throat, sealing off every gasp of air.

I couldn't breathe.

I awoke with a gasp, choking for air, the reek of smoke still thick in my nostrils. A crushing weight pressed down on my chest, pinning me to the bed. I writhed beneath it, my lungs screaming for breath, but the air wouldn't come. I thrashed, trying to turn, trying to move, to scream—to *do* anything. A broken whimper escaped my throat as I reached out blindly, patting the space where Luke should've been but I couldn't get his attention.

Still no air. My lungs burned.

Summoning the last shred of strength I had, I arched my back violently—like a feral bronco refusing to be broken— and suddenly, the weight vanished. Just like that.

I bolted upright, gasping in great gulps, tears springing to my eyes as my body tried to catch up with what had just happened.

Luke stirred groggily beside me, blinking into the shadows. "Liz?"

I couldn't answer. I could only breathe, ragged and raw, my hands clutching at my throat.

"Liz!" he said again, sharper now. "What's wrong?"

"Can't—breathe," I managed to rasp.

His eyes focused on me, wide now. He reached for my shoulders, but I was already scrambling out of bed, sobbing. "I have to get out. I have to go. I need … *air*."

I flew down the stairs in my bare feet, flung open the front door, and stumbled into the yard. I had barely made it off the porch before I dropped to my knees and vomited violently into the grass. My whole body shook. My chest heaved. I couldn't tell if it was from the nausea or the terror or both. I stayed doubled over, palms braced on my knees, trying to calm the pounding in my chest.

That's when I saw her.

A faint shimmer moved near the road—too slow to be wind, too solid to be smoke. I lifted my head, eyes stinging, and stared.

There, drifting between the edge of the lawn and the asphalt, was a pale greenish light, barely more than a flicker at first. But as it glided farther into the open, it began to take shape. The mist pulled into form—tall, slender, the unmistakable outline of a woman.

Not a woman of flesh and blood. Not anymore.

She was young, her long dark hair trailing behind her as if suspended in water. Her nightgown—if that's what it was—billowed like mist caught in motion, luminous and trailing behind her like a veil. Her entire form glowed faintly green, translucent at the edges. Not quite solid, but not air either. She looked like a memory made visible.

She moved with purpose.

She turned west, following the curve of the highway, her feet never touching the ground. Then she stopped abruptly and raised her arms above her head. She waved—slow, wide arcs, back and forth—crossing and uncrossing her arms, desperate and deliberate.

Like someone trying to flag down a car. Trying to be seen.

And then—headlights.

A truck crested the hill, engine rumbling deep and low. As it bore down the road, she didn't move. She kept waving, right there in its path.

And then—

She vanished.

But not all at once. Not like a light flicked off.

She *dissolved*, wisp by wisp, into the chrome grille of the semi—her form drawn into the metal like smoke pulled through slats. Her gown, her hair, her arms—gone. As though she had become part of the truck's passing. Absorbed by it.

I stood frozen, breath caught in my throat.

And then it came.

A deluge.

My body convulsed with sobs—deep, wracking waves of grief and panic and something more. Something ancient and aching.

I crumpled onto the lawn and wept, not caring who saw or what it meant. I wept for everything—what I didn't understand, what I couldn't escape, and what I suddenly knew to be true.

When the storm inside me finally began to subside, I became aware of Luke standing at the edge of the porch, still barefoot, still silent, just watching me.

When I turned to face him, he walked toward me slowly, cautiously. Like he wasn't entirely sure what he should do or say.

His hands pressed gently to my back, grounding me. But before I could speak—before I could explain what I saw— he met my eyes and just held them for a while.

In his gaze, I saw everything he wasn't saying yet. Confusion, deep and heavy. Disbelief that hadn't hardened into denial, just hovered there, raw and flickering. The quiet panic of someone trying to reassemble the rules of the world after watching them come undone. He wasn't ready to name what he'd seen. Not out loud. But it was there, swimming behind his eyes, refusing to let go.

"Did you see that?" I whispered, my voice barely audible. I wasn't sure if she was still out here. I wasn't sure of anything.

Luke turned his gaze toward the road. His eyes landed on the exact spot where she had disappeared.

"I'm not sure what I saw," he said finally, his voice hoarse. "I'm just... not sure." He rubbed his eyes and sank down onto the porch step, motioning for me to join him.

After I told him how I'd woken, about the dream, about the suffocation and the smoke, he was quiet. We weren't ready to talk about *her* yet. One bitter bite at a time.

"Do you think maybe it was just the dream bleeding over or maybe a bit of sleep paralysis?" Luke asked weakly.

I shook my head. "No. This wasn't that. I've read about that—this was *different*. It wasn't just pressure or panic—it was *something* pressing down on me. Heavy. Intentional. And the smoke—Luke, I could *smell* it, I could *feel* it. I could almost *see* it. It filled my throat. I wasn't imagining it."

I paused, trying to steady my voice and rubbed my arms, still chilled by the memory. "It stopped the second I pushed back. Not like I overpowered it—more like it *chose* to stop. Or maybe… maybe it realized I was aware." I looked at him. "I don't know. But it wasn't like a seizure or some sleep thing. It wasn't a dream glitch. It was… something else."

I tried to smile, my arms still folded tightly across my chest, unwilling to let go just yet. It might've been the only thing keeping me from falling apart.

He nodded slowly, then reached for a twig that had blown onto the porch and began breaking it into smaller and smaller pieces. The sound of it was soft and rhythmic. Snap, snap, snap …

"And then… what do you think that was?" I asked, my voice barely holding.
I didn't look—I couldn't—but I tipped my chin toward the street, "What we saw out there?"

He didn't answer.

He was still looking out into the dark, his brows drawn together.

I looked back toward the road, to the place where Jacquelyn had vanished.

"I think I was supposed to see her. That's why I ran outside. That's why I *had* to." My voice wavered. "Whatever was in that room with me—it didn't follow. It didn't try to stop me. It pushed me to the edge and then let go."

Luke still said nothing, but I could feel him turning it over in his mind. Trying to stitch together something that couldn't be explained by reason.

I finally worked up the nerve to look back toward the place where she vanished.

"She died running for help," I whispered. "She didn't make it. But maybe… maybe she still thinks she has to. Maybe she's still trying."

We sat in silence after that, his arm wrapped around me, my head pressed against his shoulder. I felt small.

Fragile.

Unmoored.

When I finally rose to go back inside, I switched on the light and glanced at the clock: 5:35 a.m.

Morning. Barely.

We didn't say much over breakfast. We were still inside the echo of it all, too full of questions with nowhere to put them.

After Luke left for work—reluctantly, after several promises that I'd be okay—I flipped the kitchen calendar over to April.

We'd been here just over three weeks.

And the house had begun to unravel its story—one buried secret at a time.

Chapter Eleven

I found Luke in the kitchen nights later, his laptop open on the table, forgotten. He was sitting leaning back, with his fingers laced behind his neck, staring up the ceiling like it might suddenly offer answers.

I leaned in the doorway, arms crossed. "I heard you pacing."

He looked at me. His eyes were tired. "I'm sorry. I didn't want to wake you."

"You didn't."

He stood and reached for me—steady hands, warm even through the chill in the air. "You okay?"

"I don't know," I said. "Are you?"

Luke pulled me in, held me for a moment. I could feel the quiet effort in his embrace, like he was trying to hold it together for both of us.

"I keep going over it," he murmured. "Trying to make it make sense. Rationally, logically—God knows I've tried." He stepped back, hands on my shoulders. "But I can't explain what we saw. Or what happened to you that night. Or any of it, for that matter."

I nodded. "Me neither."

He exhaled slowly. "A man's supposed to protect his home. His wife. His family. And I can't seem to do any of it."

"We can't leave. We have nowhere to go," I whispered.

"I know." He ran a hand through his hair. "I've crunched the numbers six ways to Sunday. Every cent is tied up in this place."

"The closing, the down payment," I said softly. "Ashland bought us the dream, and now the dream is a literal nightmare."

He looked at me then, and I could see the fear just below the surface—fear for me, *and* of the house. "I'm worried

169

about you, Liz. I've said it a dozen times, but I mean it. You've been through... something. And I don't know how to fix it."

"You can't fix it," I said. "But you're here. That helps." I meant that not only in the literal sense, but in every way possible. His understanding, his comfort, his belief … it meant everything.

I moved to the window then, fingers brushing the edge of the glass where condensation blurred the view of the porch. Outside, the street lay quiet, washed in moonlight. Nothing stirred. Nothing appeared. And yet…

"There are moments," I said, more to myself than to him, "when I don't feel afraid here at all. And I know that sounds insane."

Luke stayed quiet.

I turned back to him. "It's like… sometimes, the house doesn't feel threatening. Just... aware. Like it's holding its breath. Like it's expectant … waiting for something."

Luke's arms crossed tighter. "Liz, a few nights ago I woke up to you gasping for air. Your lungs were full of smoke.

You ran outside barefoot in the middle of the night. That's not nothing."

"I know," I said quietly. "I know how it sounds. But even then, even with him on my chest—I didn't feel like he was trying to hurt me. I felt like he was trying to wake me. Like he needed me to *see* something."

"Needed you," Luke repeated, almost to himself. "Like this house has wants."

I nodded. "Not wants. A need. Like it's… unfinished. Like it's waiting for someone to make something right."

He exhaled through his nose, rubbing his jaw. "You're talking like it's alive."

"I don't know what I'm talking like," I admitted. "But whatever it is, I don't think it's trying to trick us."

Luke turned toward the window, his reflection merging with mine in the darkened glass. "And what if you're wrong?"

I didn't answer. Not because I didn't have fear. But because I wasn't sure which scared me more—that I *was* wrong, or that I wasn't.

And for a moment, I thought I saw something behind us. Just a flicker.

When I turned, nothing was there.

Luke sighed and rubbed the back of his neck. "I'm going to bed," he muttered. "I've got that early call."

I nodded, and he padded down the hall, and up the stairs, his footsteps soft against the worn wood. I heard the bedroom door click shut behind him.

I stayed at the window a little longer, arms wrapped around myself, breathing in the quiet.

Maybe it was the house—its creaks and flickers and restless tension. Maybe it was the separation from everything I knew, from everyone who really knew me. Or maybe it was something more personal. The kind of disappointment you can't name but still feel watching you. Judging you.

Some days, I wasn't sure if the house was haunted or if I was.

And then there were the calls from my mother. Or more, the lack of them.

She'd only called a few times since we moved. I knew a freeze-out when I was in one.

This wasn't the first time, and I was fluent in the cold, quiet language of mother-daughter distance—delivered in tight, pleasant tones and laced with polite detachment.

Her questions on the phone were strictly surface level— weather, the house, whether or not I'd mailed the thank-you notes from the going-away party. Nothing about Luke's new role, nothing about how I was adjusting. And when I did offer anything personal, the replies were syrupy and shallow. *"Oh, good." "That's nice, Liz."* I could practically hear her disinterest humming beneath the words.

Sometimes, I'd push the red disconnect button with my hand gripping the phone tighter than necessary, blinking back sudden tears. Sometimes I wanted to shout down the silence between us. *Just ask if I'm okay. Just pretend like you care.*

I remembered the last real conversation we'd had— back when I told her we were moving.

"So. This is what you *want*?" she'd said, spitting out the word like it tasted wrong. Her eyes pinned me like a butterfly on a board.

"Yes, Mama. This is what we want." My tone had been sharper than intended, but I was tired. Tired of being measured, weighed, and always found just slightly lacking.

She didn't miss a beat. "What are you going to do if you finally get pregnant? When you have a baby? I won't be able to drop everything and come running, you know.

"And your stepfather," she added, shoving him forward like she hadn't already just taken the wind out of me, "he's not going to be able to drive hundreds of miles every time your sink clogs or you need to borrow the snowblower."

The jabs landed. They always did.

"Yes, Mother. I'm aware. We've weighed all the angles. Every way to Sunday." I tried to keep my voice steady. "We know there are downsides, but this is a good opportunity for us."

174

At that, I caught the eye roll she *almost* managed to hide. I let it slide.

"It's a big promotion for Luke," I added, quieter now. "With a big raise. We could use the money."

But I was already shrinking into that too-familiar feeling—small, defensive, ten again.

Then she raised a hand. End of discussion. "It's your life, Liz. You do what you want."

A timer had gone off in the kitchen then. The oven, signaling dinner. A clean break, like the bell ending a round. And just like that, the fight had been over. No knock-out, no winner—just more bruises and more silence.

We didn't talk about it again. Occasionally, I caught the glint of quiet disapproval in her eyes, but she held her tongue. And I let it go, too. Peace, however uneasy, felt easier than another round.

But now, sitting in what was supposed to be my dream home turned haunted house, I couldn't help but wonder if she'd been right.

Maybe I *was* too soft to leave Ashland. Maybe, after living my entire life in the same small town, I was more dependent on its predictability and my family than I realized. Like a convict who forgets how to breathe fresh air after too many years in a cell. Maybe I wasn't as free here as I thought.

Maybe the cage I'd just stepped into had prettier wallpaper—but it still locked behind me all the same.

Chapter Twelve

I flung the book softly onto the kitchen table just as Luke sat down for dinner. It landed face down at his place.

He smiled at me before turning it over. "What is this, my love?"

His expression changed the moment he saw the cover: *Real Ghost Stories of Lancaster County.* A prickle ran up the back of my neck, like it did when I first saw the title, and I imagined he felt the same as he held my gaze, then slowly opened the book.

I stood there watching him, the dinner pot and ladle poised in my hand, as he searched my face.

"Go ahead, open it," I said. "I dog-eared the page for you."

Luke flipped easily to the marked spot. I turned back to the stove and began ladling the stew into our waiting bowls.

The Lady of Lincoln Highway

Limeville, Lancaster County

If you find yourself driving along Route 30 in the pale hours before dawn—especially near the stretch that cuts through Limeville—keep your eyes on the road.

And whatever you do... don't stop for the woman in white.

Long-haul truckers have whispered about her for years. A pale figure, barefoot and drenched in mist, appearing suddenly in the middle of the highway. She raises her arms, slow and deliberate, waving them over her head like she's trying to flag someone down.

They say if you swerve to avoid her, your rig might jackknife off the road. And if you don't—if you drive straight through—she disappears the second you pass her. Not all at once. *In pieces.* Wisps of her trailing behind, vanishing through your grille like smoke.

No one knows exactly what she wants. But everyone agrees on this:

She's looking for help.

The story isn't ancient. It's not one of those passed-down-for-generations folk tales. No, this one's newer. And much closer to home.

It began on the morning of May 8, 2007, just before sunrise. A fire broke out in a modest house along Lincoln Highway during a home renovation. Investigators later discovered a construction worker had unknowingly hammered a nail into a live electrical wire inside the new addition. It smoldered in the walls for hours—quiet, hidden—until it erupted just before dawn.

That morning, neighbors would later recall hearing distant sirens—but by then, it was already too late.

When firefighters arrived, they found signs that someone had tried to fight the blaze from inside. Faucets had been left running. Wet towels were stuffed beneath doorways, blackened at the edges but not consumed. A man's body was found in the hallway, overcome by smoke.

But his wife wasn't in the house.

She had made it out.

She had run—barefoot and in her nightgown— into the smoky predawn light, trying to flag down help.

That's when a tractor-trailer came barreling over the hill.

The driver never saw her until it was too late. He told police he'd looked away—just for a second—to take in the sight of the burning house. When he turned his eyes back to the road, she was already in his headlights.

He hit the brakes. Hard. But she disappeared beneath the wheels.

She died just feet from her front lawn.

Some say she doesn't know she's dead. That she's still trying to get someone—*anyone*—to stop.

Others believe she's caught in the moment just before impact. Trapped between the fire and the road. Between the life she had and the one that was taken.

Truckers still report seeing her in the mist— same place, same time, always just before dawn. Even the ones who drive that route every week say the hair on their arms rises when they pass Limeville. The ones who've seen her swear it's not a trick of the light. They say her gown shimmers green, like something pulled from the bottom of a deep lake. They say her face is blank. Or burned. Or sometimes… it's looking right at them.

And the house? Still standing. Barely.

One family tried to move in years after the fire. The charred addition was rebuilt. The lawn was mowed. Curtains were hung.

They barely lasted a month.

When asked why they left so suddenly, they refused to speak. The property went dark again. And it stayed that way.

This author has tried to reach those occupants for comment.

No luck. They don't return calls.

But people in town have a theory. They say no one can live in that house anymore because — it's already full.

So if you find yourself driving through Limeville before sunrise...

Keep your hands on the wheel. Keep your eyes ahead.

And if you see her—don't stop.

Not unless you're ready for her to follow you home.

When Luke finished reading, he slowly closed the book —but left it face down, still open to the story. His hands stayed folded in his lap. He stared at the cover, unmoving.

I waited.

Finally, I broke the silence. "Well? What do you think? Sensationalized, I know, but crazy … right?"

He didn't answer. Just shrugged—small, defeated. He looked like a man who'd just opened a box he'd spent years trying to keep shut.

I wanted him to say something. Anything. I didn't want to carry this alone.

"I found that at the library today," I said, walking over to the island and grabbing a stapled bundle of papers. "Along with these."

He flipped through them without much enthusiasm at first—just skimming. But I saw his eyes narrow, his focus sharpening. These weren't more campfire stories. They were news clippings.

Man Perishes in Fire, Wife Dies Seeking Help

May 8, 2007 – Lancaster, PA

A fire that broke out in the early morning hours on Lincoln Highway left both of the homeowners dead. Ryan Taylor, 35, perished inside the house. His wife, Jacquelyn Taylor, 34, escaped the blaze, but was struck by a passing tractor-trailer while attempting to flag down help.

Truck Driver Not Charged in Tragic Death

May 20, 2007 – Lancaster, PA

Lance Kugler, 49, a driver for Har-Quil Trucking Company, struck Jacquelyn Taylor just minutes into his route. "I saw the fire first," Kugler stated. "Smoke was blowing right into the road. I looked away for just a second—and when I looked back, she was there." Authorities confirmed wind conditions and visibility contributed to the tragedy.

Obituaries – May 11, 2007

Jacquelyn M. Taylor (née Garmen), 34, manager at Irene's Quilt Shoppe and beloved Sunday School teacher, is survived by her parents, siblings, and extended family.

Ryan M. Taylor, 35, a surveyor with Crocker Engineering, was known for his work in the church and community. A joint celebration of life service will be held Friday. Interment will be private.

He kept reading—through fire department statements, investigation updates, an op-ed about the haunting. One article confirmed the cause of the fire: a hot wire nailed into during construction. It had smoldered for hours before erupting. The towels, the running sinks—it all lined up with what we'd read. What we seen.

The last page in the packet was about the house itself. Since it had garnered such attention from the stories that emanated from it, someone had delved into the history and decided to publish it.

It had sat empty for years. The dead couple's families had inherited the property but couldn't agree on what to do with it. Aside from mowing the lawn and sealing off the ruined addition, the house had been left largely untouched until 2017. That's when it was finally sold to a family from Philadelphia, who restored the addition and moved in—only to vacate a few weeks later. No public statement. No explanation. Just... gone.

Luke turned the last page, letting it rest now face down on the pile. He was quiet again, but I could feel the shift in him. Something heavy settling behind his eyes.

He still hadn't looked at me.

He sat with his elbows on the table, fingers laced tightly, his gaze fixed on the worn, dog-eared cover of the ghost story book. His jaw was tight, shoulders drawn in like he was bracing for something. Something he couldn't quite name.

I watched him try to process what he'd just read—not just the campfire tale, but the real reports. The names. The photos. The burned house that was now *our* house. The woman we had seen.

Finally, he exhaled—slow, shaky. "So that's it, then." His voice was low. "We're officially living in the middle of a ghost story."

I didn't respond. Not right away.

He leaned back in his chair and rubbed his face with both hands. "Jesus, Liz."

"I didn't make it up," I said quietly. "It's all there. I found it at the library. It's real."

"I didn't say you made it up," he said, but his tone was clipped. He stood abruptly and walked to the window, pushing aside the curtain and staring out into the dusk.

There was a long silence.

"I'll admit, I thought at first maybe you were losing it, imagining things," he admitted, his voice flat. "But when you woke up choking that night — when you ran outside and saw someone — I saw her too."

He turned to face me, finally. His expression was raw. "Liz, I *saw* her."

I nodded. "Jacquelyn," I whispered.

He looked haunted. Not in the ghostly sense—but in the way of someone realizing the foundation beneath their life had just completely cracked open.

"And Ryan," he added. "He died trying to save the house," he repeated.

Our house.

He didn't need to say it. We were both thinking it. We were living in a house where they built their hopes and dreams. Where they might have argued, or laughed. And where they planned a life they never got to finish.

Luke dropped back into his chair. The packet of articles lay in front of him, he opened it again to the two obituaries printed side by side.

"She was just trying to help him," he said. "And he stayed to save what they were building. It almost has a ring of 'The Gift of the Magi' to it," he mused.

What he said tickled something in the back of my brain, "It's as if they were both doing something for each other, and that need wound up in tragedy. And now it's like they're both got stuck in that moment," I said softly, starting with a tickle of realization. "They never got to finish it. Never got to find each other again."

I pulled another thread of an idea I had researched. "Did you see what time they all said this happened, Luke?"

He shook his head and perused the articles again, "They all just mention just before sunrise."

"Yeah, and at that time of year, the sun rises before 6 a.m. in Lancaster. I looked it up."

"So, what are you getting at?" He asked.

I thought it was obvious. "Every time we've woken up to something, it's been about 5:20 in the morning. You typically start seeing the first peeks of light about a half hour to one full hour before actual sunrise." I let it sink in.

The room felt heavy.

"I don't know what to do with this," he said. "How do we live in a place like this?"

I didn't have an answer. Not yet. But I knew one thing.

190

"We're already living in it," I said. "We just didn't know the whole story before."

"And now that we do?" He posed.

"What if he's reliving the fire every day, trying to *do* something. Maybe he realizes now, it's not the house he needs to save, but her."

Chapter Thirteen

I waited a few days before returning to Shelly's house, the weight of everything I'd learned settling heavily on my chest. Anna had told me her husband had been there that night —on the fire crew, a firsthand witness to everything I'd only begun to piece together. I wasn't sure what I expected from Shelly exactly, but I knew this much: I needed to know everything I could.

She opened the door before I even knocked, her eyes already scanning my face.

"You look like you've seen a ghost," she said, the old cliché landing with more weight than it typically deserved.

I gave her a half-hearted smile, "Something like that."

We sat again at her kitchen table, lemon-scented cleaner lingering faintly in the air. This time, I came armed. I pulled the library book from my bag—**Real Ghost Stories of Lancaster County**—and set it gently on the table between us. The pages were marked, worn now from being read and reread.

Beneath it, I placed the packet of news clippings I'd found. Obituaries. Fire reports. The haunting story of Jacquelyn and Ryan Taylor laid out in grainy print.

"I found this at the library," I said. "And... " I hesitated, letting my voice trail off.

Then in a rush, before I could stop myself "I think it kind of confirms a few things I've seen.

"Things I've felt."

I waited for her to react, but Shelly didn't flinch. It told me all I needed to know. She picked up the book, flipped to the page I'd dog-eared, and scanned the opening lines in silence.

"I thought of you," I added. "Because Anna told me... your husband may have been one of the first responders that night." I wanted it to come out less accusatory. I didn't want her angry with Anna.

At that, Shelly looked up. Her expression softened. She nodded slowly.

"Thomas was on the crew that morning," she started, her voice soft. "He was just a kid back then. Barely twenty. But he's never forgotten it." She hesitated, then stood and walked to a small cabinet in the next room. From the top shelf, she pulled down a worn leather-bound notebook, the kind that looked like it belonged to another era.

"I talked to him about you after you left last time. He said you'd more than likely be experiencing … things. He told me I could show you this."

She slid it across the table. "He used to write short stories once in a while as a way of journaling some of the stuff he saw. It's only about eight pages. You can stop when you get to the page with the paperclip."

She held the journal open, and I took it from her with a trembling hand. The ink was dark, steady. The handwriting neat and unadorned. I began to read.

Date - May 8, 2007

I felt the alarm pulse through me long before I heard it—a whisper at the edge of my brain, like a faint tendril of a half-remembered dream, curling its way into my consciousness. It wasn't unusual for me; I'd grown accustomed to that primal awareness, the deep instinct that stirred in my bones when the call came. My eyes flicked open, and I turned toward the clock. 5:25 a.m. My body moved automatically, the same fluid motions I'd learned to rely on while on call. I leapt out of bed, already fully clothed as was my habit, ran my fingers through the tangled mess of my hair. I rubbed the sleep out of my eyes, flicked my tongue over my fuzzy teeth, and grabbed my shoes before heading straight for the door. As I stepped outside, I squinted toward the east, already spotting the rising plume of smoke in the distance. The faint glow of an orange sky hinted at the fire's origin.

The fire station was further west, and it would be a few minutes before I knew for sure. I slammed my truck into gear, flicking the siren's light on top, the bright whirling beam cutting through the pre-dawn stillness. I hit the gas and the tires crunched over gravel, sending stones scattering in all directions as I rushed onto the street. The urgency felt familiar, the weight of the unknown ahead pressing on my chest like a cold hand.

When I arrived at the station, the team was already gearing up, adrenaline starting to pulse in the air, thick and heavy. The chief's voice cut through the chaos as he briefed us. A house fire on Lincoln Highway, he said. The owner had called in the fire himself, refusing to leave. His life savings had been poured into a new addition, and now he was trying to save it. "Great," I thought bitterly. "A moron playing hero." My stomach turned at the thought of how we might be forced to risk our lives to save his.

But there was more. A woman had been struck outside the same house by a semi-truck. The speculation was she'd run out to flag someone down for help, but now she lay motionless in the street, her life cut short in the blink of an eye.

At twenty, I was still a Red Hat, a rookie, so I was assigned to Engine 1, a 1980 Mack.

The engine snarled beneath us as the old Mack tore down the road, and I could feel every gear shift in my chest. I was in the jump seat, strapped in but still gripping the edge like it might steady my nerves.

The sirens moaned and warbled, the lights spiraling in a mesmerizing pattern, casting long, distorted reflections on the leafless trees. The adrenaline began to buzz through me, my heart picking up its beat in sync with the engine's roar.

It felt like an eternity to reach the scene, despite it only being about two miles from the station. The semi traffic was light this early, but a few trucks lumbered slowly out of the way, pushing us to our limit in the race against time.

We arrived within minutes, the first responders on the scene, ahead of even the state police. As we rolled up, the flickering lights of the ambulance in the distance were the only comfort I had, though it did little to quell the gnawing unease prickling just under my skin. I was the first to spot her—her body lying motionless on the road, a grotesque tangle of twisted flesh and torn fabric. For a moment, I couldn't even tell where one ended and the other began.

Her body, crumpled on the street like a broken rag doll, was twisted in ways no living thing should be. Her arms were bent backward, unnaturally at the elbows, and her legs jutted out at freakish angles, as if bent by hands unfamiliar with the limits of flesh and bone.. The skin of her neck was stretched taut, almost too thin, from her spine being pulled out of alignment. Her face—her poor, mutilated face—was frozen in a grimace, her features contorted with an agony I could almost feel in my own soul. It was like the body ceased to be human, crooked and mangled beyond recognition and I felt my stomach twist painfully.

I tried to shake the image from my mind. I'd been trained for this. Blood, injury, death—it was part of the job. But something about this scene made my chest tighten, my breath hitching in my throat as I stood frozen for a second. Was I going to be sick? I took a few deep breaths, forcing my lungs to expand, trying to focus on the task at hand.

We knew there was nothing to be done for her. There would be no miracles here. We covered her with a fire blanket from the truck and left her for the EMS to handle as we turned our attention to the fire. It was a moment I'll never forget—the sound of the reel creaking and whining as the heavy length of hose spilled out, the noise filling the silence, almost like an eerie soundtrack to the chaos unfolding. I wanted to look away, but I couldn't. Part of my mind still clung to her, still wondered if there were pieces of the story I wasn't understanding. Why had she run out there? Was she trying to save someone?

Maybe her husband had sent her out here in the dead of night. I shuddered at the thought, realizing I'd just made an unintentionally bad pun.

Adrenaline surged through me as we prepared for the fire. The familiar rush hit my veins, my heart racing, my breath quickening in anticipation. But still, my eyes kept drifting back to the twisted shape of the woman on the road. I couldn't stop staring, unable to make sense of it.

Then, something happened.

I turned back toward her, the strange pull of something—some instinct—compelling me. A flicker of green light rose above the blanket, barely noticeable at first, like a glow from a far-off candle.

But it intensified, shimmering like an ethereal mist, rising higher and higher into the night air. The light coalesced, transforming into something solid, something unmistakable. It was the shape of a woman—her body, perfect and sculpted, like clay molded by an invisible hand, a tattered nightgown billowing around her delicate frame, and long, dark hair floating in the air around her. She hovered just above the road, everything defying gravity. Her gaze fixed straight into mine, her arms stretching out before her, palms open, as if she were pleading for help. Her head tilted slightly, and for a moment, time seemed to stop, the world holding its breath.

I stood frozen, locked in that gaze, my limbs stiff, my lungs struggling to take in air. The silence between us stretched on, heavy and oppressive. And then, without warning, her head snapped back violently. Her body shuddered, vibrating as though caught in an unseen tremor, and then—just like that—she disappeared. Not in the way she had appeared, but in a sudden, bone-chilling zap, like a television screen being snapped off.

I blinked, disoriented, looking around at my squad mates, at the other emergency workers, the onlookers. No one else seemed to notice anything. They were all focused on the fire, the next steps in trying to quell the raging flames. No one had seen what I did. It was as if I had slipped into a different reality, one where I was the only witness, the only one who had seen her. A part of me felt detached from the world, as though I were watching a movie, a grotesque joke playing out before me. But it didn't fit with my nature—my logical, analytical mind screamed that this couldn't be real.

I shook my head then, as though the simple motion could wipe the image from my mind, and focused on the task at hand. The hose was ready, and we moved forward, farther down the gentle slope to the home. I never looked back.

The fire was a Class C, ignited by a live wire—an unusual but devastating incident. It had smoldered for hours before finally catching, only to erupt in the still of night. The addition had been sealed off, and by the time the main house's smoke detectors went off, it was already fully involved. The husband, as we later discovered, had stayed inside, trying to save the addition. He didn't make it. The wife had likely been sent out for help, but it was too late. At least, that's what the chief's investigation concluded.

By the time I reached the end of the entry, I was shaking.

I placed the journal carefully on the table still opened to the last page, and just stared at it for a long moment, letting the silence stretch. My throat was tight, and my voice came out thinner than I expected.

"That's what I saw," I whispered. "Exactly. Almost every detail."

Shelly didn't speak. She let me find the words.

"Her nightgown. The long hair…The way she *appeared*. I thought I imagined it. Thought I was having some kind of breakdown. But this—" I tapped the open page. "He saw it too. All those years ago."

She folded her hands together, watching me with a stillness that said she knew I still had more to say, more to process.

"She's reliving it," I said, a germ of something sparking alive in me. "That moment. Over and over. She never got to finish what she started. She never reached help."

I felt tears rising before I could stop them. I blinked them back, swallowing hard.

"And Ryan," I added. "He's still in the house. I think he's trying to wake someone. I think… I think he's trying to find her, like he never got to finish what *he* started. To save the house, their dreams, her."

Shelly reached across the table and placed her hand gently on mine. It was warm and steady.

"Then maybe," she whispered, "it's time somebody finishes it for them."

Chapter Fourteen

The box had been sitting on the kitchen counter for a few days, untouched.

I'd moved it there with the intention of going through it again—of making sense of what I'd found, of piecing together who the people were that were in the photos. But every time I lifted the lid, the scent of old paper and faint woodsmoke made my throat catch. It felt sacred somehow. Like I was rifling through someone else's memories without permission.

That morning, I stood over it in my robe, fingers brushing the soft edges of it, when the idea struck me—Anna.

She knew this town in a way I didn't. She'd lived here for forty years, raised her family here, probably couldn't go most places without someone recognizing her and vice versa. If anyone could help me recognize the rest of the faces in those photos, or recognize the significance of the sprig of forget-me-nots, the locket — it would be Anna."

I tucked the box carefully under my arm and started the short walk down the street.

When I arrived, Anna was out by the garden beds, wearing her wide-brimmed hat and gloves, gently hand-tilling the soil, readying it for whatever she was going to plant.

"I brought something," I called as I trotted down the gravel driveway.

She looked up, squinting in the sun, then smiled. "If it's more zucchini seeds, I'll have to start making anonymous bread deliveries."

I laughed, holding the box easily in my right hand as I walked over. "It's not seeds. It's… something else. From the house."

Her smile faded just a little, replaced by something quieter. Curious, maybe. Cautious. "Come on back to the porch," she said, pulling off her gloves.

We settled in with iced tea. The sun was bright and the breeze was soft, stirring the wind chimes. They answered with a soft, wandering melody—high and hollow. For a moment, I let myself take her in—noticed the quiet details I hadn't registered before — Her calm presence. Her hands, always busy. The way she'd kindly accepted me — even when I'd shown up at my worst, without question or judgment. A warm ache settled in my chest, one I hadn't quite named yet.

"I found this in the floorboards in the living room," I said, lifting the lid. "I think it belonged to them. The couple that died in the fire. I think …" I wasn't sure.

Anna's gaze dropped to the box. She set her glass aside and reached in, gingerly lifting the photographs from the top.

She went through them once in silence. Then again, slower. On the third pass, she paused, held a photo toward me, and pointed with her left hand.

"That's Ryan Taylor," she said softly. Then she tilted the photo to the light. "And that beside him is Jacquelyn. She was a pretty girl."

She didn't sound surprised. Just… settled.

"I thought it might be them," I said quietly. "But I wasn't a hundred percent sure."

Anna nodded, still studying the photo. "I used to run into her at the quilt shop when I'd go in to get fabric and supplies, and we'd chat. You always remember the ones who leave an impression. She was kind. Always had a way of making you feel like she had all the time in the world."

She reached for another photo, this one of the couple in wedding garb, with two other people, a small bridal party. "That girl there," she said, pointing to the brunette in a green dress, "I'd guess she was Jacquelyn's maid of honor. She didn't have sisters—just brothers, if I remember right. So that must've been her friend. I think I used to see her around the shop, too.

"But the man, that's Ryan's older brother, Jason. They looked a lot alike, except Jason had lighter hair. He worked at an auto shop on Millersville Road for years. It's closed now."

I looked at her. "You knew them pretty well."

She shook her head. "Not as well as I would've liked. Just...it's a small town. You notice things. Especially when you've been here long enough. And, honestly, I thought we had time." She smiled a wistful smile, and then went back to the photos.

She then pulled forward the photo of Jacquelyn gently cradling her barely rounded abdomen. Her fingers trembled slightly. "So she really was pregnant when she died," she whispered. "There were rumors, but nothing was ever confirmed."

She turned the photo over. "There's no date on this one, but she looks about the age she was when it happened. She was so young, poor thing."

She pressed a hand gently to her lips and closed her eyes. I noticed her hands then—pale, almost translucent, her knuckles like small river rocks, worn smooth with the passage of time.

She studied Jacquelyn's face for another long moment —then looked back at me.

Then she did something unexpected. She lifted the photo and held it up beside my face, her eyes narrowing, mouth parted slightly in disbelief.

"The resemblance really *is* uncanny," she murmured, almost to herself. Then to me, with a bit of hesitation, "Surely you've seen it too?"

I nodded. "It completely freaked Luke out when I showed him. He thought I was messing with him."

She lowered the photo, voice softer now. "That's why I acted so strange that first day. When you showed up on my porch. It felt like she was standing there again. Like I was seeing a ghost."

"I think Ryan... I think he reacted when I pulled that photo out. I was in the kitchen. The air changed. The kitchen shook. Honestly, it was like a cyclone blew through there."

Anna's eyes widened slightly, but she didn't question it.

A long silence stretched between us. The weight of recognition settled heavy on the table between the box and the photographs.

Then, almost absently, I reached for the dried forget-me-nots I'd kept pressed between the folds of cotton fabric—

something smaller, quieter, easier to hold than all that had just passed.

Anna smiled at the sight of them. "That would've been Jacquelyn, alright. She planted them over there. You'll see. They'll come up soon. They were ground cover for the beds over there. She loved them. She used to tuck them in greeting cards. Said they meant something, although I'm not sure what that was."

"And this?" I held up the small silver button, with the etched viney pattern on it, "Do you know what this is? If it held any significance to anything?"

Anna's eyes studied the detail as she rolled it over in her fingers. "Hmm. I don't know. Perhaps it was something she brought home from the quilt shop. Maybe she was going to use it for a project." She handed it back to me and I put it back in the box, carefully. Wondering. If they kept it, it had to have some meaning.

A hush settled between us.

"They didn't just lose each other," I said quietly. "They lost their future, too."

215

Anna reached out, placed her hand over mine. "And maybe," she said, "you were meant to find that, to honor their past."

I went home after a pleasant visit with Anna, forgetting the contents of the box for a while as we sat and chatted amicably about everything under the sun.

I pulled out my laptop and sat at the kitchen counter and just out of curiosity, did an internet search: F*orget-me-nots meaning*. And wouldn't you know, the answer was as soft and blue as the flower itself. They're a symbol of remembrance. Of holding on, gently. Of saying, *I haven't forgotten you,* even when time tries to blur the edges.

Some site said they were once carried by lovers parting ways, a promise in petal form. Or tucked into letters meant to outlast time. Another called them a sign of enduring connection —between people, between memory and the heart. Tiny flowers that bloom low to the ground, year after year, like they don't want to be noticed, but insist on staying anyway.

And I don't know—something about that got me. That quiet insistence. That idea of being remembered not with noise, but with something soft and constant.

Chapter Fifteen

We waited for days. After reading Thomas Yoder's account of what he saw—what he *wrote*—I could barely sleep. The image of her rising from her own body haunted me, not just because it matched what I'd seen... but because I couldn't shake the feeling that *he* was still here, searching.

We never seriously considered ghost hunters or mediums. No cameras, no sage sticks, no dramatic rituals to post online. The idea of turning our house into a spectacle—of inviting strangers to poke and prod at our grief and confusion —felt wrong.

So we made a quieter plan.

No lights, no Latin. Just me.

It was Luke's idea, mostly. He thought a man's voice might come across as threatening, too forceful. He was afraid it might provoke... something.

And maybe he was right. Maybe whatever was here needed gentleness. A softer approach.

218

So I would be the one to speak. To reach out. Carefully. Deliberately.

To try.

So I gathered the things I'd found under the floorboards: the stack of letters and cards, the **Mother Goose** book, the wooden box with the photos and the pressed forget-me-nots. A little offering of memory, of recognition. A message of my own.

And then, just before dawn, the smell came back.

I sat bolt upright, heart racing. The thick reek of smoke choked the room, curling in at the corners, familiar now but no less terrifying. I reached across the bed and shook Luke awake.

Before he could speak, I pressed a finger to my lips and pointed toward the far side of the room.

He understood immediately. He sat up, shoved the pillows behind his back, and stilled himself. He barely breathed.

I slid out of bed and into the plan we'd agreed on.

"Ryan?" I said softly. "Ryan, are you here?"

There was no reply. Just the thick, acrid scent hanging in the air like a held breath.

"I can smell you. I think you're in the bedroom," I continued, careful with my words. I didn't want to imply it was *our* space. It wasn't—not to him.

We were the intruders here.

"Ryan? Can you let me know you're here?"

Still nothing.

My voice trembled a little now. "I need to talk to you. Please. Just give me a sign. Anything."

The curtain twitched.

Not from a draft—but a pull. Intentional.

Luke and I locked eyes. He gave me a nearly invisible nod, then sat frozen, doing everything he could to appear small, still, safe.

"Was that you, Ryan?" I asked, my voice tight. "Did you move the curtain?"

Another tug. Slow. Deliberate. Like a performer easing the stage curtain open.

"Thank you," I whispered. "Thank you for that."

I hesitated and then steadied myself and went for it.

"What do you need, Ryan? What can I help you with?"

Silence. Then the curtain fell closed.

"Ryan?" I said again, more urgent now. "Are you still there?"

I sat down on the bed beside Luke. He tilted his head toward me like he was asking, *Abort?* I shook my head. *Not yet.* I held up my finger: *Give me a moment.*

"Ryan," I tried again. "What do you want? Why are you here?" My voice rose with the urgency of the question.

And then it came.

The breeze.

Soft at first—just enough to lift the ends of my hair. But it grew quickly. The smoke thickened, and the air in the room began to pulse.

"He's upset," I whispered. "I think I said something wrong."

"Ryan," I said gently, "I know you're frustrated. I know you're trying to find something. Or someone. Let me help you."

The breeze became a wind. The pages of my book flipped wildly. A framed photo tipped off the dresser and shattered on the floor. Luke flinched.

The tension snapped in me.

"Ryan," I said sharply, "Stop. Stop this right now."

A vase on the dresser toppled before it pitched across the room, grazed my cheek and landed in shards, sprayed across the floor. I gasped, staggered back—then something *really* hit me. Not something I could see. But a force, strong and invisible, lifting me like I weighed nothing and flinging me straight across the room.

I slammed into the wall and crumpled to the floor.

I didn't hear Luke scream my name. But I felt it.

It was like everything dipped underwater—the way sound bends and slows when you sink.

"LIZ!" he called. I could hear the panic under his voice, the helplessness. "LIZ!"

I couldn't answer.

And then I heard him.

Luke. Not talking to me—but to him.

"Ryan! Stop it! You're hurting her!" His voice hoarse with emotion.

And just like that—the wind stopped.

Everything fell.

Books. Glass. Papers. They all dropped from mid-air like gravity had suddenly remembered them.

Silence. Only the lingering smoke remained.

Luke was at my side in a heartbeat. He gathered me into his arms and rocked me, whispering my name. I felt the warm pressure of his hand on the back of my head, the tremble in his chest.

And then I heard it.

A squeak.

Soft. Rhythmic.

Then another.

It was a sound from another life. Familiar in the way dreams are familiar. A fingertip dragging across glass.

Writing.

That's what it was.

I blinked slowly, still half-dazed, as Luke's head turned sharply toward the sound.

He knew it too. The sound was unmistakable.

It was a message.

Written in soot and fog, in long, careful strokes by an invisible hand.

We both stared as the letters formed—slowly, precisely.

JACQUELYN

Luke exhaled, almost in disbelief. "Thank you," he whispered, his voice breaking.

"Thank you, Ryan."

He helped me to the bed, clearing debris with one arm while steadying me with the other. He fluffed a pillow and settled me back.

I put my fingers to the sting on my cheek. My fingertips came away sticky with blood.

"I think it's okay," Luke said softly. "It missed your eye. Not too deep. I'm more worried about that bump on the back of your head. I'll go get some ice."

I nodded absently, my gaze locked on the soot-smeared letters — still fresh, still shimmering in the condensation, still etched across the window.

Luke returned and lightly pressed the ice to the back of my head, while he settled in beside me.

Jacquelyn.

Her name.

"Why would he write her name?" I asked quietly. "After everything... that's what he chose to say? We know her name.

"Why now?" I whispered.

Luke exhaled slowly beside me. "Maybe he's trying to tell us something about her. Or... maybe he's looking for her?"

The words lodged somewhere behind my ribs. *Looking for her.*

I blinked, and suddenly the photos in Anna's hands came rushing back—Jacquelyn laughing at a backyard picnic, them dancing together, holding her belly in a soft, maternal gesture. And Ryan's face beside hers, always turned toward her. Always watching. Always adoring.

"He died in the house," I said slowly, my voice unfamiliar. "She died outside."

Luke nodded. "Right. So maybe he didn't see it happen."

"He might not even know she's gone." The air thickened, and my chest tightened like something invisible had wrapped around it.

And then it hit me. Hard. Deep. Unforgiving.

"Oh my god," I breathed. "He's been waiting for her. This whole time. He's been *waiting*."

The realization slid in slow and cold, like water seeping through a cracked foundation—silent, but impossible to stop. My arms prickled with goosebumps. My eyes burned.

"And every time someone else moves in," I said, my voice hollow, "he thinks maybe it's her. Maybe she's come back."

My hands were trembling now. I pressed them together to make them stop.

"But it's not her. It's never her."

I felt the old floorboard shift beneath us, like the house was listening. Like it *knew*.

"And when he realizes it's strangers—again—"

"He lashes out," Luke said.

"Because he doesn't understand," I whispered. "Because in his mind, she left and didn't come back. And then everyone else took her place. Over and over."

A wave of sorrow curled through me, slow and cold. I remembered the dream. The weight on my chest. The smoke in my lungs.

"He's not trying to scare us," I said, blinking fast. "He's grieving."

Luke was quiet.

And I—God help me—I hurt for him.

"And maybe…" I hesitated. "Maybe it's worse with me. Because I *look* like her," I whispered,

Luke nodded slowly, a chill passing between us like a draft from the attic.

"He thought she came back," he whispered back.

"Only to realize I wasn't her." I finished.

And then it started to make sense. All of it.

I thought of the mantle, the broken picture frames—to him, just frames of strangers' faces.

"The broken photos," I said. "The ones he smashed our first week here. He didn't recognize them."

Luke followed my gaze. "Because we weren't supposed to be here."

I turned to him, the pieces falling into place. "The furniture we kept finding moved. We thought it was just random."

"But it wasn't," he said. "He was rearranging it. Trying to make it feel like it used to. Or just trying to get rid of what didn't belong."

The image made my throat tighten. I thought of the boxes we found opened in the living room, our things rifled through, edges smudged with ash.

"He was searching," I said. "In everything."

Luke's eyes widened a little, and I could see he was with me now—seeing it, too.

"The smell of smoke," I murmured. "It's not just a reminder of how he died. It's... it's him."

"And his presence," I whispered. "Reaching out. Trying to hold onto whatever's left of her."

"He was trying to wake me at the time of the fire. That's why I felt that compulsion to get out of the house." I was trying to piece it all together.

I let that sit for a minute.

The smell of smoke had started to fade, but the weight of it still clung to the room. To me.

"He wasn't angry before," I said. "Not like that. Not until I asked what he wanted."

230

Luke glanced over at the broken glass on the floor, the overturned lamp. "Do you think he thought you were asking the wrong question?"

"Maybe," I murmured. "Or maybe I got too close to the right one."

I turned my eyes back to the window, to her name written in that soot and silence. And then I said it—soft, with a certainty I felt in my bones, aching with possibility and mused again,

"He's been searching for her. All these years."

Luke didn't speak. He just squeezed my hand.

And somewhere in the fog, even through the throbbing in my head and the ache in my ribs, a thought began to form.

A plan.

Chapter Sixteen

It wasn't the alarm that woke me. It was the smell.

Faint at first—so faint I thought I was dreaming—but then it thickened around me, edged with something scorched and metallic. Smoke. Not the comforting kind from a chimney. The other kind. The kind that we had come to understand … he was here.

I sat up fast, my heart already thudding in my throat. Luke was awake too. Sitting on the edge of the bed, shoulders rigid, staring at the closed door like he expected it to open on its own.

"He's here," he said.

I nodded. "It's time." We had deliberately waited for this day, this date: May 8. The anniversary of that fateful day.

We moved without speaking. Every motion felt ceremonial—deliberate, reverent. I reached under the bed and pulled out the wooden box. It had lived there for weeks now, collecting all of the things we knew they'd left behind. Pieces of their life together. I clutched it to my chest for a moment. It felt warm. Or maybe I was just cold.

The hallway beyond the bedroom door was dark—too dark. Like the kind of dark that doesn't just fill a space but claims it. I stepped into it anyway.

"Ryan?" I called softly. The windows rattled.

The air shifted around me. I couldn't see him, but I could feel him. That pressure. That sorrow.

I looked at Luke, who stayed just behind me. Always behind me. Steady, even now.

"We're not here to force anything," I said aloud. "But we think… we think she's waiting for you."

A creak echoed from the end of the hall. My body went still. I reached into the box and pulled out the quilt square, the one that held the tiny flowers—a simple piece of cotton. I laid it on the floor just outside our bedroom door.

"You left this behind," I said, my voice barely above a whisper. "Maybe you meant to. Or maybe you didn't know how to take it with you." A wind whipped up bouncing off the walls of the hallway. I steadied myself against the wall, but kept moving forward. I stepped onto the landing. Each step measured. I laid another object on the top stair, one of the cards from Ryan to Jacquelyn.

I didn't hear it, exactly—I *felt* it. The air behind me shifted, like something old and broken had just found the strength to move.

I held my breath and clung to the banister instinctively as a force from behind surged and I felt myself start to tumble off balance. I caught myself on the step below, and turned to face the air behind me, "Ryan. Please trust us. We know what you've lost. We want to help you find her."

The house seemed to shift again, not like something settling, but like it was telling another piece of the story it had been aching to finish. Floorboards groaned. The breeze leapt up the stairway.

Smoke curled past me again—brushing my cheek, teasing me. I didn't flinch this time. I just let it pass through me.

We took another step. And another. With each one, I placed something from the box. A quilt square, a button, a letter, a sprig of flowers. Each piece a memory. Each one a whisper: *You're safe. You're not alone. We remember.* Waiting each time to feel the weight of it shift with that hush in the air, that subtle pull of a soul remembering the promise that kept it tethered.

Behind us, the air crackled.

"Come on," I said gently. "You're almost there."

We reached the bottom of the stairs. I placed the photos one by one between the bottom of the steps and the front door, ending with the one of her pregnant.

Luke had gone ahead, so the front door was open now. Just a crack. The porch light had burned out sometime in the night, but a faint lavender glow bled in from the horizon. Sunrise was coming. It was 5:19 a.m.

I stepped onto the threshold and laid down the last object just outside the door: the box itself. The same box that had held all the fragments of a story too painful to tell. The same one that had sat like a time capsule under those

235

floorboards for decades. I opened and placed the key inside it so he could see. So he would know.

The house groaned one final time.

Then I felt him—right next to me. Close enough to chill the air. Close enough to hear the unspoken question: *Why now?*

I turned toward the porch. "Because today's the day," I whispered. "This is when it happened. And this is where it ends."

The wind picked up. Only here—not in the trees, not across the yard. Just on the porch. The chimes started to trill out the bones of a lullaby. And then, from somewhere else came another sound. Not metal. Not glass.

A hollow, echoing ring, like breath skimming the rim of fine crystal.

My chest tightened.

I took one step off the porch into the yard. The air felt different now—charged, expectant. I looked to the road. Still quiet. Still dark.

And then… there she was.

She rose like mist from the pavement, green-tinted and softly glowing. Her hair floated around her shoulders. Her dress fluttered without wind. Her hand lifted.

She didn't speak. She didn't need to.

Jacquelyn.

I felt Ryan surge behind me, like a current finally reaching the end of a wire.

"She's here," I said, and stepped aside.

For one long second, the entire world paused. Time folded in on itself. I saw both of them then—not in full color or clarity, but with my heart.

He moved past me—across the porch, down the steps. The air around him shimmered, and for the first time, I could see him. Not clearly. Not fully. But the *suggestion* of a man, flickering like film catching the light of an old projector. As if the past itself were trying to remember him.

He reached the middle of the yard, and for a moment, I thought he might hesitate again. But then Jacquelyn stepped forward from the street. I swore I heard her name uttered on the wind. It came out as air, as light, as relief.

They met in the middle.

I didn't blink. I didn't breathe.

They didn't embrace. Not physically. But the way they yielded to each other—the soft lean, the surrender—the light around them turning warm and gold—it was enough. Their edges blurred, already fusing into the same stream of light.

And then I saw it.

A twinkle—small, sharp, impossibly bright—flaring between them.

And the thought came again, unbidden, clear as day: *And baby makes three.*

And then, they were gone.

The light collapsed into morning. The wind fell still. The house behind me gave one last creak, then settled, completely quiet for the first time in months.

Luke wrapped an arm around my waist. I hadn't realized I was shaking.

We didn't say much when we stepped back inside.

There was no need.

The air felt different now—like something had finally let go. The weight was gone, lifted from the beams and boards.

For the first time, the house felt still. Peaceful. Ours.

Ours.

After I gathered the photos—tucking each one gently back into the box, along with the locket, the dried sprig of forget-me-nots, and the folded love notes—I closed the lid and held it to my chest.

Only then did I let Luke lead me upstairs, the early light just beginning to seep through the windows. My skin still hummed with what we'd witnessed. There was something electric in the way he looked at me—like we'd just returned from the edge of something ancient and unknowable, and the only language left was touch

We closed the bedroom door behind us, and let the world fall away for a while.

Later, wrapped in the hush of early morning, I lay still, listening to the house settle. But this time, there were no shadows at the edges, no whispers beneath the walls. Just warmth. Just peace.

No more unfinished business. Not here.

And for the first time in my life, I understood something that had always felt just out of reach.

My father hadn't left me.

He'd only changed form.

He had moved into the quiet places—the invisible spaces I'd never known how to name.

Into the pull of the current. The soft lapping of the lake as it kissed the shore.

The hush between tree branches.

The low, steady drum of my own heart.

He hadn't vanished. He had become *everything still and constant.*

He had been with me the whole time.

And one day—when my hour comes—I will see him again.

But not as the girl with the tear-streaked cheeks, begging him to stay.

This time, as his grown daughter—

a woman who has made peace with the silence.

Like a prayer I didn't know I'd been whispering my whole life.

A woman who now knows that love doesn't vanish.

It transforms.

It tethers.

It yearns and …

It waits.

Epilogue – May 2023

Liz watched her like a hawk. While she was so pleased that Ryanna loved coming to Anna and Bob's and seemed to have no fear of the water, she set about putting the life vest, swimmies, and SPF 70 on her as soon as they walked into the backyard.

Today, Ryanna had announced that she was ready to jump off the dock—the same dock that had already seen many decades of joyful kids' feet.

Liz and Anna sat amicably chatting in their lawn chairs by the edge of the water, lazily sipping their iced teas and watching as the four-year-old ran off the dock, squealed, splashed, and then paddled back to the ladder as fast as all the flotation gear she was sporting would allow, ready to begin the sequence all over again. Each time, Dex, their chocolate lab—now three years old, and every bit still a puppy—followed his best friend off the dock and into the water, happily paddling behind her.

Liz reached up absently and brushed her fingers over the golden locket at her collarbone—the one she had found in the box, tucked beneath the old photographs and folded cloth. It had been empty then, but so clearly kept for a reason. Saved. Meant for something.

Now, it held two small photos—one of Ryan and Jacquelyn, their smiles still soft and full of possibility, and the other of Ryanna, wide-eyed and laughing, her sweet, dark curls barely contained in the frame.

Liz wore it every day. A thread between what had been and what still was.

Sometimes, in the hush that followed Ryanna's delighted shrieks, Liz's thoughts strayed to her own mother—the brittle smiles, the quiet guilt, the love that always felt like a test.

Distance hadn't fixed that story, but it had stopped it from writing every chapter. Here, with Anna's steady warmth beside her and Ryanna's bright future in front of her, Liz finally understood the shape of the mother she wanted to be: one who saw her child, not her own reflection; one who offered room to breathe, not reasons to shrink. Her own childhood would stay —a cautionary tale, not a blueprint.

Ryanna Jacquelyn Barton had been born February 8, 2019, at 5:20 a.m.—two days before her due date, but exactly nine months after Ryan and Jacquelyn had been reunited. Liz was almost certain they had conceived on that very morning, as she and Luke had physically celebrated the reunion, completely wrapped up and buoyed by the hope the two lost souls had given them.

A faith enduring.

A hope everlasting.

And love since time immemorial.

What burns may fade, but it is not lost;

Even ash carries the memory of fire.

I am the ember, hidden and patient,

Smoldering quietly in the hearth of your heart.

You will not see me—but you will feel me,

In the crackle of sorrow, in the warmth of remembering.

Death took only the shell of me.

What matters was left burning in you.

THE END

Book Club Discussion Questions

Themes & Emotions

1. "Making it right" is a recurring phrase for Liz. How does this need affect her choices—and is it ever fully satisfied?

2. Grief and longing show up in multiple timelines. How does the book suggest we carry—or release— those we've lost?

3. What role does the house itself play? Is it a character, a symbol, or simply a setting?

4. How does Liz's infertility struggle connect to the haunting? In what ways are the two entangled emotionally or metaphorically?

5. Do you think there's a moment when Ryan realizes he's dead? If so, when—and what clues led you there? If not, how did that ambiguity affect your experience of his story?

6. How does the possibility (or impossibility) of Ryan's awareness shape your understanding of the

haunting—and of Liz's role in helping him move
on?

Characters & Dynamics

7. Jacquelyn never speaks, yet her presence is deeply
   felt. How does the novel give her voice without
   words?

8. How do Shelly, Anna and Carrie serve as foils or
   mirrors for Liz's experience? What truths do they
   help uncover about grief, healing or connection?

9. Ryan attempts to reach out—to Liz, to the Miller
   child. Is he seen as a threat, or something else? How
   do your feelings about him evolve?

10. What did you think of Luke's role in Liz's emotional
    journey? Supportive partner? Bystander?
    Something more complicated?

11. How does uncovering of the past change Liz's view
    of the present—and her future?

Style & Symbolism

12. The novel is rich with quiet symbols—the smoke, broken photo frames, the locked box and its hiding place under floorboards, the forget-me-nots, a peaceful landscape that contrasts the turmoil inside. Which image or symbol stayed with you, and what do you think it represented for Liz—or for the story?

13. How does the novel balance the supernatural with the emotional? Did one element stand out more to you?

14. Were you satisfied with the resolution? What questions lingered for you after the final scene?

Which Embers Character Are You?

(Best done with wine. Or something stronger if your faucet just turned on by itself.)

1. When something feels wrong in your house, you...

A. Light a candle and journal your feelings

B. Blame the plumbing

C. Investigate immediately, flashlight in hand

D. Assume it's your fault and try to fix it

E. Pretend it's fine but secretly Google "signs your house is haunted"

F. Invite the ghost to tea and ask what they want

G. Start baking. If you're going to be haunted, you might as well be polite.

2. Your emotional armor of choice is...

A. Sarcasm

B. Silence

C. Over-functioning

D. Intuition

E. Logic

F. Softness as strength

G. Hospitality (and a backup pie)

3. What's your relationship with the past?

A. I carry it like a backpack

B. I dream about it

C. I left it in a box somewhere

D. I'm trying to understand it

E. I live next door to it

F. I'd resurrect it if I could

G. I make peace with it—and then make pie

4. Choose a ghostly aesthetic:

A. Smoke curling up from floorboards

B. An open window that was definitely shut

C. Water running with no sound of footsteps

D. Footprints across ash

E. A pie cooling on a windowsill that no one made

F. Nursery walls painted in soft green

G. A heartbeat echoing through old wood

5. Someone you care about is spiraling. You...

A. Try to make it right, even if it breaks you

B. Watch from the edge, not sure how to help

C. Step in and hold things steady

D. Share what helped you and hope it lands

E. Gently ask questions until they hear themselves

F. Stay close, even if they can't see you

G. Wrap them in warmth and feed them something healing

6. How do you feel about second chances?

A. Desperate for one

B. I missed mine

C. I'm working on earning it

D. I gave myself one

E. Cautiously optimistic

F. Not for me

G. I believe in them—quietly, completely

7. Pick a sound you can't explain:

A. Floorboards creaking under no one's feet

B. The front door unlocking itself

C. A baby crying in the distance

D. Water dripping when all the faucets are off

E. Wind whistling through a closed window

F. A whisper in a room that should be empty

G. A kettle whistling before you ever turned it on

Results

Mostly A: LIZ

You carry grief like a compass and try to fix what can't be undone. You're determined, haunted, and hopeful—even when you don't believe it yet. You don't run from the past—you walk into it.

Mostly B: RYAN

You're the ache that lingers, the protector who stayed too long. You want to be seen, to be heard, to be *understood*. Letting go feels like betrayal—but maybe it's mercy.

Mostly C: LUKE

You're the steady presence who doesn't ask for much—until the ground shifts beneath you. You want to understand, even when the answers scare you.

Mostly D: SHELLY

You've walked through fire and made peace with the ashes. You carry your story with grace, and when someone needs a hand, you offer one. Not because you forgot your pain—but because you forgave it.

Mostly E: CARRIE

You notice things. Things others miss. You don't need to be loud to be powerful. You're the one who sees the truth before anyone else does—and asks the question no one else is brave enough to say out loud.

Mostly F: JACQUELYN

You're memory and presence, comfort and ache. You are the ghost who loves too much to leave. You've become something eternal—still warm, still watching, still waiting.

Mostly G: ANNA

You believe in the sacredness of a warm welcome, and you're nobody's fool. You've seen things, felt things, and know that comfort and courage often go hand in hand. When the world starts spinning, you're the one who says, "Come in. Sit down. Let's talk."

Acknowledgments

Endless thanks to Becky, Dina, Kristen, Beth, Sue, Dave, and Dan— You read with care, questioned with kindness, and helped me find the beating heart in the middle of the story. I'm so grateful for each of you.

To my son, Dan—For being kind, for keeping my sanity in check with your neverending humor, for encouraging me without hesitation, and for reminding me that love shows up in the quietest ways. Sharing our arts—your music, my words—has been one of my favorite parts of this process. You've taught me the value of giving thoughtful feedback and the grace it takes to receive it. I'm grateful for both. You are truly one of my greatest joys.

To my husband, David—Thank you for indulging every late-night horror flick, for chasing me around clapping like we're in a game of *Hide and Clap*, and for pointing out the mundane moments—a clock's tick, the dog's nails clicking across the floor, a random soulless tune—that might just make the perfect horror scene. Most of all, thank you for being the kind of love that even time can't dim. The kind I'd find again and again, no matter how many lifetimes it takes.

About the Author

Rowan Kade is a writer from Pine Forge, Pennsylvania, whose work explores the quiet spaces where grief lingers, memory slips, and ghosts press in from the edges. She appeared on the literary scene only recently, though her stories feel like they've been waiting a while. Her writing is drawn to old houses, unspoken histories, and the emotional hauntings we carry with us long after the funeral ends.

Embers is her debut novel, a meditation on loss, legacy, and what it means to finally let go. She lives with her husband— and perhaps a few uninvited guests.

Rowan is currently at work on *Traces of Limeville*, a companion novel told from the other side of the fire.